Sign up for our newsletter to hear
about new and upcoming releases.

www.ylva-publishing.com

OTHER BOOKS BY EMILY O'BEIRNE

A Story of Now Series

A Story of Now
The Sum of These Things

Points of Departure

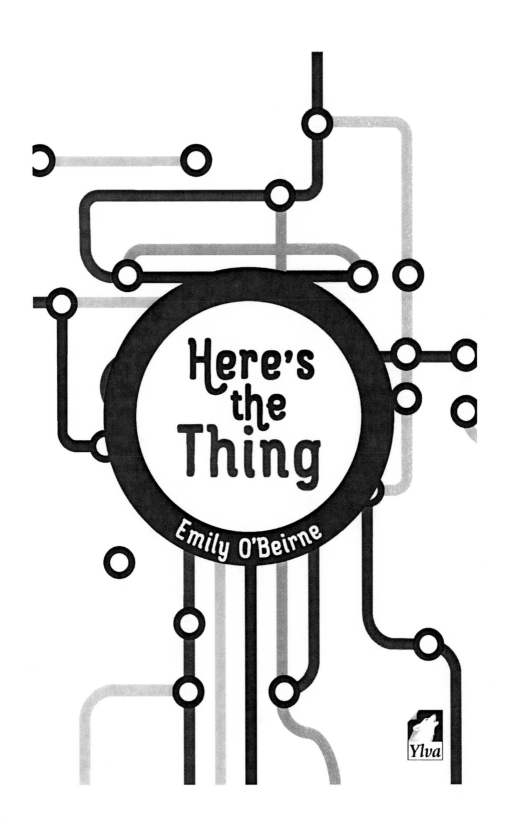

Here's the Thing

Emily O'Beirne

Ylva

DEDICATION

This story is dedicated to a book called *Emma Who Saved my Life* and to its author Wilton Barnhardt. His story, discovered in my teen years, launched many a subway journey for me for me and is the inspiration for Zel and Prim's adventures in this book.

~ ~ ~

She still sends me pictures. They pop up on my phone every now and then, these silent reminders of her.

Or sometimes they arrive by the snail trail of the post. I'll find the thin envelope sandwiched between bills and real estate letters addressed to the last tenants. And when I break the seal, my heart beating a predictable storm, there'll be a single photograph, slid between the sheets of flimsy envelope paper, the image unmarked by its long journey. But instead of feeling that little thrill I used to when she sent me pictures—because it meant she was thinking of me—it just hurts.

I file them away in a desk drawer, where I don't have to look at them but can feel safe in the knowledge that they exist.

We used to do it all the time, send pictures. Not of each other or ourselves. Neither she nor I are the type for that kind of navel-gazing crap. We took photos of randomness, sent only to amuse: a close-up of a cafeteria French fry looking unlike any known food; a spectacularly stupid scribble on a toilet wall; an old man in girls' sweatpants at the bodega. It was how we narrated the story of our day to each other, back and forthing with images of our minutiae. We didn't post them for everyone else to see. We weren't trying to stage our existence like so many kids at school, glossing their lives with the right hashtag and filter. It was our own private conversation.

These days I send her words. I send her words because I desperately need them back from her. But she only sends those same pictures. She refuses to change the terms. And even though I'd love to grab her and shake her, I also know she's just doing what she always does, studiously ignoring whatever she doesn't want to pay attention to.

But it's not fair. Because on that day at Coney Island, the terms did change. And now I need her to *talk*. I need her to explain her sudden lack of ways to say things. I need her to explain why she's never online when I am. Why she didn't come to meet me that day we were going to Far Rockaway. Why she's disappeared, all but for a few pictures in the mailbox. Pictures that make her silence more profound, not less.

And I keep writing, hoping something will rub that silence raw, open a wound. And then maybe she'll be forced to release words from that human fortress she builds.

CHAPTER 1

As soon as she hears the words "New York", the blonde princess perks up.

"You actually *lived* there?" Her voice is still measured, but I can hear the hint of intrigue. Suddenly I'm worth something. She straightens her blazer, looking curious and a touch self-conscious. Like the mention of that city has chafed at the all-comforting sense of superiority she held a second ago when she sized up my loose-haired, loose-jeaned, couldn't-give-a-crap eyeliner look. Now her perfectly braided hair, subtle eye make-up, and her prefect's badge don't stand a chance against me (well, New York). It's like she suddenly feels like the boring provincial cliché she is.

Please don't think I'm a bitch, describing this girl like that. I'm not a bitch. Really, I'm not. It's just that you weren't here ten minutes ago. I swear it was surreal. She was nice as pie when Mum was here, making small talk, telling us about the school excursions and clubs and extra university prep courses they offer. Then, the minute Mum went in to chat with the senior school coordinator, she went on this total backspin from perky polite to general disinterest. All before the office door even closed.

Of course, that was before I uttered the four, golden 'lived in New York' words. Now she's all ears.

So excuse me for judging, but you have to admit it's kind of deeply shallow on her part. Like something out of a bad teen movie. She's one of those popular girls, all shiny and judge-y and awaiting her comeuppance, the one who underestimates the new girl at the start. This, of course, casts me as the nerdy but likeable girl. The one who'll either seek revenge on all the high-definition girls like this evenly tanned overachiever next to me or else become wildly popular by getting a makeover from a gay man, making some excellent quips, and then dating from the girl-clique's private male gene pool property.

Believe me, people, when I say that NONE of this is going to happen. What *will* happen, if Mum and Dad magically convince me go to this school, is that I will put my head down and stay as invisible as humanly possible. Because if she is a taster of the school social menu, I plan to officially bow out of all interpersonal efforts.

We've already taken the full tour of the school and grounds, led by the blonde, in chirruping prefect mode, and the principal's assistant. Apparently this school's so exclusive that potential Golden Ones don't even get to meet the principal until they're properly signed on, fees paid. Together they schooled Mum in everything this place has to offer. Because she'll be the one paying the fees for the Olympic swimming pool and the sky-lit art rooms, right? And while I dragged my feet behind them, I didn't get a chance to find out if all the other students are carbon, depressing copies of this one either. All the girls (yes, only girls, which you would think would make me happy but it actually doesn't) were tucked away in the classrooms. But my guess is, given the North Shore location and the amount of zeroes I saw on the fees list, that this sample of blonde *wayyy*-upper-middle-class Sydney sitting right here is probably representative enough for me to turn and run for the hills. Or at least back to the inner west.

"Like, New York, New York? Not the state," the girl asks, wrinkling her nose slightly as if she can't imagine that hallowed city allowing rabble like me in. Which, of course, shows how little she knows about the place. If she thinks I'm rabble, she's got another thing coming when she and her fake designer suitcase finally make it there. If New York knows how to do anything, it's how to produce prime rabble. It prides itself on it.

"Yes, the city," I say patiently instead of sighing the sigh of the withering, which is what I really want to do. If I were Prim, I probably would have. I'm the kind of person who can manage to stay on the right side of polite, but Prim's got zero tolerance for girls like this. But then, Prim's got zero tolerance for most people. "We lived in Midtown."

The girl looks blank.

"It's the middle of Manhattan, near Times Square," I explain as two girls in uniform, looking just like this one but brunette and *sans* prefect badge, peer into the office. One says something, and the other cackles as they pass. I shudder. Get me out of here. Now.

Blondie perks up some more. "That's where they have the New Year's parade?"

I nod.

"Did you go?"

I fight the urge to roll my eyes. I wouldn't be caught dead there, fighting for a square inch of space with a gazillion tourists and out-of-towners. The parade is what television is made for. It's for parents and old people and the rest of America to watch while New York goes out. Prim and I had planned to spend New Year's Eve planning our New World Order. I don't have time to fill you in on the details right now, but let me tell you this much—this girl here would have trouble surviving once we run the show.

Before I can respond, Mum is finally ejected from the coordinator's office. I'm so relieved to see her I have to stop myself from jumping up and hugging her. She gives me a thin smile like she, too, has been to private school hell and back.

The coordinator is right behind her. She's a shaggy middle-aged woman wearing a pastel sweater dress straight out of the eighties. Now I really feel sorry for Mum. Ten minutes in the presence of that outfit is probably pushing at the edges of human endurance.

"I hope to see you next week, Zelda," the coordinator says to me. "Meaghan will show you back to the gate, won't you?"

Blondie McPerfect nods enthusiastically and leads us back to the car park full of shiny Land Cruisers and zippy hatchbacks. She chatters all the way, practically igniting with excitement when she hears Mum's line of work. I smirk to myself. It must be killing her that two such unimpressive-looking people's life CVs are impressing her so much.

I tune out and watch the school go by. The playing fields are movie-set green, the sprinklers keeping the summer sun from doing its worst. That'd be right. Last night's news said parts of the Blue Mountains are ablaze with bushfires, but North Sydney is lush.

As soon as Meaghan leaves us with a wave and a faux-friendly *see you next week*, I turn to Mum. "I'm not going here. No way."

Mum kind of clicks her tongue, but it's half-hearted too, like she feels just as out of her element. She knows that just because we can afford schools like this monstrosity now doesn't mean we belong to them.

But just in case she wants to argue, I go on. "For starters, I cannot be wearing that dress. You and I both know pink and green does absolutely nothing for me," I say in my best snooty voice.

Mum unlocks the doors and chuckles. That's what I love about Mum. Even if we have enough money, and even if in her secret wannabe heart she'd love for her daughter to attend a school like this, she also knows it's not really me or her. Or Dad either. Or anyone we know, really. We'll never be like those people. Never *want* to be.

"Okay," she says wearily, yanking open the car door. "We'll talk to Rosa about Antony's school."

I nod, trying not to grin too hard. My cousin Antony's school is one of those inner-city places with cool teachers and a strong arts game. It's also got a great academic reputation too (otherwise Aunt Rosa wouldn't have even let Antony darken its doors). I don't know why we didn't just go there first. I guess we were a bit curious about the posh school. Now I am most definitely not.

Minutes later we're driving back to the safety of the inner west, where the world makes sense and I can breathe without inhaling all that gross pretension. I scrutinise Mum's face, checking she's not still hanging onto that 'one of best schools in Sydney' dream.

"You know I can't do a place like that," I say. "Don't you?"

She lets down the window a little and nods. "It's probably a bit…stiff for you, I know. But I wanted to see if maybe you'd like it. We can afford it now. And it would get you into any university course you wanted."

I nod, breathing in the blend of traffic fumes and fresh sea air that has come to mean Sydney for me. "I know. But I just want to go to a normal school with normal people. Not a place packed to the rafters with bland catalogue models and pristine everything. It's boring."

Mum grins at the catalogue comment. I definitely know how to metaphor my way into my mum's frame of reference. She nods. "Okay, we'll go see Rosa tonight. We've got a little time."

I sigh and tip my head back against the seat. A week. A week until I have to start school. And for the thousandth time since we got here, I wish we were back in New York. I even wish for the stuff that I hated at the time, like struggling through the crowded sidewalks and freezing air to my ratty school three blocks away. Like the obnoxious smell of the laneway under our fire escape. Like the creeper who owned the bodega across the street from us. It's better than getting used to everything all over again.

After eight months, New York had just started to feel like home. And even though it was smack bang in the middle of the most famous city in the world, it became my normal. And now it's gone. And if I have to leave our flat and my photography classes and the subway project—and Prim—I at least want to be at a school I don't hate.

CHAPTER 2

"Go on." Aunt Rosa points at the front door of their miniature terrace house. "Go show your cousin around Sydney."

I trail Antony down the narrow footpath. My cousin's gotten even taller. He's wide too. Not fat, just thick. And he kind of lurches as he walks, his hands tucked in his front pockets, his thick black helmet of hair falling forward. It's like his head, or maybe his brain, is leading, steering his body where it wants to go. It's a weird and endearing combination of clumsy and businesslike.

He doesn't stop walking, or even say anything, until we get to the water fifteen minutes later. Then he flaps a hand at the harbour. "Opera house," he mumbles.

I grin and fight the urge to let out a big fat "duh". And it's even harder to restrain myself when he points out the Harbour Bridge. I don't, though. He's my cousin, even if I haven't seen him in years; and he's had it kind of rough lately. Besides, I kind of like the perfunctory nature of his tour guiding. Bare minimum sightseeing.

I mean, I'm not that excited by a bridge, or a building that looks like plates stacked on a dish rack anyway. Once you've seen pictures of famous places, you've seen them, right? Like, how exciting could the Eiffel Tower be in reality when you've seen it a thousand times on posters and in movies?

Sights pointed at, Antony clearly decides his job is done. We march back to Surry Hills and stop at a tiny café sandwiched between a skate shop and yet another café. This one is teeny and wood-trimmed and cute as hell, with its hanging plants and colourful Tupperware. Nearly every table is full. I hunt down an empty one outside and look around at the outfits and haircuts. I'm sniffing some definite hipsterville.

Once he's got a flat white in hand, Antony brightens up. By which I mean he actually speaks to me. "How long are you here?"

"A year at least. How've you been?" This wouldn't usually be such a loaded question, but this time it is. His dad, my Uncle Ant, died of a heart attack eight months ago. He was only thirty-eight. And since then, it's just been Antony and Rosa and Madi, his little sister.

When Ant died, Rosa had to go back to teaching, and it was hard for them for a while. It was hard for Dad too. He really missed his brother, and he was frustrated that we were so far away and he couldn't help Rosa. His other brothers were around to help. (I've got a *ton* of uncles on Dad's side. Um, okay, so you should also probably know I can be prone to exaggeration—it's more like four.) But as the oldest, Dad felt bad for being away.

I haven't seen Antony since it happened. I don't know if I'd survive if either of my parents died.

"I'm fine. Mum and Madi are okay. It's all fine. We're coping." He sounds like he's reciting something off the back of his hand. I stir sugar into my tea and watch him watch the group of kids at the next table as they pass around a phone, laughing at something onscreen. Then he looks back and shrugs at me. It seems to say, *I don't know what else to tell you.*

I nod and dutifully change the subject, getting straight to the second most pressing topic. "So, what's your school like?"

Mum and Rosa are talking about the school right now. I have a feeling that by the time we get back, I'll be going there, so I want the lowdown, *stat.*

"It's good. Lots of arts, less sports. Which means less rugby wankers." He sips his coffee. "And that's fine with me."

I smile. Fine with me too. Organised sport is *not* my thing. And beefsteak rugby players? Definitely not my thing.

"And there's no school uniform either," he says.

I perk right up at that. After this week's whirlwind web tour of posh inner-Sydney schools, I've seen enough colour variations of pinstripes and plaid to last me for years. I'm perfectly happy to jeans it for the rest of my education.

I listen to him talk about the school in his slow, proper way and remember how much I like my cousin. Antony used to be our family's "problem child". According to Aunt Rosa, anyway. When we were kids, he was really super quiet and he wouldn't talk to anyone. Except me. I didn't see him that much, but when I did, I *made* him talk to me.

I remember hearing the grown-ups talking about him. There were whispers of things like autism and Asperger's tests. But Mum told me later that the doctors told Rosa he was just your everyday, non-specific socially awkward and to let him catch up at his own pace. That was tough for Rosa and Ant to stomach, I think. They were so loud and social, and they loved to have dinner parties and barbecues all the time. Then here was this kid who'd barely say 'boo' to anyone for his first twelve years.

When he first started high school, he went to a Catholic boys' school, but they let him change in Year 9 after a shitty year of bullying and macho boy crap. I could have told them it was the worst place to send him.

Don't get me wrong. Antony is definitely a geek of the all-out variety. But he's also perfectly happy existing in his geekdom. Like, if someone called out his insane levels of nerd to his face, he'd probably just shrug and say nothing. He doesn't aspire to be any different, and I'd bet money he has zero secret aspirations to climb any kind of social ladder. That's one of the things I love about him. He quietly does not give a crap. And I think he's at the kind of school now where it's easier to be that way.

"So, what subjects are you going to do?" he asks.

"Not sure. I have to match what I was doing at my last school. English, History, Bio, Psych. Art, maybe? Do they have French?"

"Don't think so."

"I guess I'll pick something else."

"You should do Drama with us."

"Drama?" Rosa told Mum that Antony is into theatre stuff now. I wouldn't have picked him for a drama kid. He's so...still. "And who's 'us'?"

"My friends. Drama's great at this school." He drains his coffee. "So's our teacher."

I think of the stupid little musicals my old school back in Canberra used to put on, all dancing and singing and embarrassing costumes. Not my thing at all. I tell Antony as much.

He shakes his head. "No, it's not like that. Peter puts on a big school play every year to make the parents and the principal happy, but the class stuff we do is way cooler."

"I'll think about it."

He nods and folds his arms over his chest. "So, how gutted were you to move here?"

"Pretty gutted. It's such an awesome thing for Dad, though."

Did I tell you that part? That Dad is the reason we moved here? He got offered this amazing contract in Sydney for a year, and Mum was about to finish in New York, so they decided it was perfect timing. I, on the other hand, did not.

When we get back to Antony's house, Mum and Rosa are sitting around the kitchen table with Anthony's yearbook and catalogues around them. Mum looks up at me, and I know it's decided. And I can see relief in her eyes, like she knows I'm not going to argue this time.

She points at the catalogue. "Come look at this."

CHAPTER 3

I spend the Monday before school starts hanging around our new house in Glebe. There's nothing else to do. I don't know anyone, and I don't know the area. Dad says I should go out and explore, but I can't be bothered. Besides, I still miss New York and Prim, and it's hard to get enthusiastic about *another* new place.

Mum's home too, supposedly settling me in. But what she's really doing is mainlining coffee and working frantically from home on the back deck, laptop on her thighs, preparing to start her new job at the Sydney agency.

Yesterday, Mum and Dad dragged me to Glebe Markets. It was kind of cool. It's a little flea market set up in a primary school, full of all kinds of food and crafts and second hand stuff. I found a cute green shirt and put it straight over my tank, unbuttoned, to protect me from the Aussie sun. I'd forgotten how brutal it is. Mum bought a plant to hang in the sunroom window, and we ate sugary crepes as we wandered the leafy streets back to our house. The sky's so blue and the air so sweet smelling it's nearly enough to make me happy to be here. Nearly.

I drag myself out for a walk. Mostly because I'm sick of my bare new room but still too lazy to decorate it yet. Exploring a city is no fun without Prim's dire imaginings to make everything seem like an adventure even when it's not. She loved to point out people or places and think of the worst, grossest scenarios possible for them. I don't know how well she'd do here. Sydney doesn't really lend itself to that kind of creepy imagining. It's too sunny and big-skied and normal.

I plod down the hill and turn down a random side street, nearly bumping into a woman walking four tiny dogs, all mismatched breeds with matching polka dot scarves around their necks. Then I notice she's wearing the same scarf. Total Glebe eccentric. I wish I had my camera with me as I skirt the pooch parade and keep walking, the breeze blowing warm over my bare arms.

In New York, it's freezing right now. I think of Prim kicking trails through the icy slush in Bryant Park and frowning into the steely winter sunshine. *It's only a year*, I tell myself. Then maybe we'll get to go back. Unless one of my parents' careers gets in the way *again*. Why did I have to be born to such overachieving parents? Especially when I'm such a normal, regular achiever? Not under, but definitely not over.

I always thought when we came back, it would be to Canberra. That's where I used to call home. Not that this is something to boast about. Canberra's kind of like Sydney's boring great aunt, the one you have to invite to Christmas because she never married or had kids of her own to torture on holidays. The one who gives you terrible Christmas presents, like an illustrated children's Bible atlas or a sewing kit.

Suburban Canberra is particularly dire. But I didn't really notice until I was older. When you're a kid, anywhere can be exciting. You make your own fun. So, even though we lived in the beige-brick suburbs, with their rows of matching houses and identical streets, I was never bored. There were parks everywhere, and the footpaths were wide and flawless, perfect for biking and skating and hanging around with all the other kids that roamed the hood. We only went inside for dinner and homework. It wasn't until I was fourteen, when I started realising that maybe I wanted a life beyond my own nature strip, that I actually noticed I was living in a cultural void. Not that I ever thought I'd get to live in New York. That definitely came out of nowhere.

Suddenly the world was huge. Almost *too* huge. When we first arrived, I stuck close to the few city blocks around our apartment, only exploring further with my parents on weekends when we did the tourist stuff like the Empire State Building and the Bronx Zoo.

A lot of kids at my school stuck to their neighbourhoods too, needing nothing outside the few blocks where their apartments and schools and friends existed. And I probably would have done the same if it weren't for Prim and the subway project. But that wasn't until later.

I turn down another street. Glebe is what you'd call eclectic, a random mix of terrace cottages and sprawling weatherboard houses. It's that time of day in Sydney when the sun's thinking about setting and everything goes a bit golden.

It's kind of beautiful. That's the thing. No matter how homesick for New York I feel, I can't help liking this city. Sure, it can be crowded and cranky like any big city, but it's also gilded and sun-drenched and stunning. Here the sky's so big you feel insect-small, and when it's not peak hour, the air smells good, like sea salt and gum trees. And there's always room to move. In New York, everything's up way too close yet totally impersonal at the same time. And the smells? That's a cocktail I could've handled never getting to know. Still, I'd go back there in a second. I would. Even if I had to put up with the worst of the summer's-day-garbage-in-an-alley smell for the rest of my life. Even if it was just for a minute, I'd still go back there and put myself right in front of Prim. Then she'd have to talk to me.

I know what you're thinking. I know you're sitting there thinking this is one of those stories that starts with the main character yanked out of her regular, happy life in a cool place, forced to live somewhere remote and weird where she knows no one. She totally hates it at first, but by the end of the story, she's all transformed and learns to love it and wants to stay forever. Well, let me tell you right now: this is not going to be one of those stories.

What I will do here is what all the heroines in the novels do. I will *endure*. I will live through this year because I love my dad and I'm proud of him and because I'm not a brat child. Meanwhile, I'll enjoy some sunshine and the mild winter and maybe even this new school that sounds a lot less uptight than my old one. But the whole time, I'll be hoping that we're going back at the end of it. Because home is where Prim is.

~ ~ ~

I get the feeling that a few folk, just like my blonde prefect friend back there, might get some misguided idea that my life is exotic or something. Just because I used to live in New York. Or maybe thinking that I'm some rich brat who gets to travel all the time.

Nope, it's not like that at all. Like I said, until I was fifteen, the only place I'd ever lived was Canberra. Hardly a high-flying cosmopolitan existence, right? We're not rich, and we're not exactly glamorous. In fact, we're pretty typical middle-of-the-road Aussies. I eat toast with Vegemite for breakfast (I'm a more butter, scraping of veg girl) religiously, Mum's guilty pleasure is *Neighbours* (now, can you please instantly forget I told you that?), and my Dad's favourite food is ribs from the barbecue. My parents just happen to have glamorous (sounding) jobs, which means I just happened to live in New York for a year.

We moved there for Mum. She started a model agency years ago with a friend in Canberra. She used to be a casting agent, but then she started model booking. I know, I *know*. But it's *so* not as glam as it sounds. Mum spends most of her days on the phone, wrangling clients and drinking enough coffee to razz an elephant. Anyway, she ended up selling out of the company because she said it was too hard for it to grow in a small city like Canberra. Mum *loves* her job as a booker, though. She's really good at it too, which is why a friend helped her land a job with this really big company in New York for a year. They loved her so much there that when Dad got his job here, they offered her an even better spot at their Sydney office. And she took it, she said, because Dad moved to New York for her and the least she could do was move to Sydney for a year. Notice no one's doing anything for me in this equation? Yup, trying not to be bitter.

Anyway, I'm happy she landed this job, but I'm still praying they take her back in the New York office at the end of Dad's contract.

People always ask me the same three questions about living in New York.

Question one: Was it amazing? Well, yes and no. It was definitely kind of mind-blowing at first. I couldn't get over the size and the crowds. And I also remember how weirdly *familiar* everything seemed. I would walk down some streets and think I'd been there before, which is impossible. That's how much American TV and film we see in Australia. Like, sometimes I'd be walking down the sidewalks and there'd be crowds of people and cars and that steam that rises up from the grates on the street (which I always thought was fake). I'd feel like I was on a movie set. It was *so* surreal. Then it just got kind of normal. There were definitely things that weren't amazing too. There was the constant peak hour. There were the bad smells and the constant noise. There was the cold in winter and the heat in summer.

There was the lack of space too, on the street and inside. Our apartment was tiny. We did a house swap. So while we lived in the middle of Manhattan, this guy and his son lived in our three-bedroom house back in Canberra. We won out on location, but they definitely got the sweet end of the space deal. My bedroom barely fit a bed and a set of drawers. I had to do my homework at the kitchen counter.

Question two: Was it dangerous? I think that's all the movies and TV shows we watch. It didn't *feel* that dangerous. I wouldn't walk around in the middle of the night (even if my parents let me), but I wouldn't do that in Sydney either. There were definitely places on the subway project where Prim and I went that made me feel uneasy. Prim probably did too, though she'd never show it.

Question three: Did you see/meet any celebrities? No. God, I hate this question. And what would it matter if I did? It's not like I was going to march up and chat to them about their latest movie, anyway. I saw some girl I recognised from a TV show once, but I did what any sane person or New Yorker would do and stared surreptitiously from a distance.

Basically, living in New York City was pretty normal. At least it was until Prim came along. When I met her, it became a different place. It became even bigger. It became a place to be discovered. It was exciting.

CHAPTER 4

I ended up choosing Drama in the end. Mostly because it worked some sort of timetable magic, giving me the last two periods on Thursdays off. And for the sake of a half-day, I decided to trust Antony that this class would be okay, even if I'm not exactly the theatre type.

When I find the classroom, a few minutes before the bell, it's already nearly full. These kids are eager. We're in one of those portable classrooms, the type they install when there are more students than school buildings. It's way out back, jammed between the science labs and the teachers' car park. I wonder if the teacher takes it personally.

Inside, all the tables and chairs are pushed back against the wall, and everyone is either perched on the edge of a table or sprawled on the floor. Afraid to negotiate the terrain of limbs and books between me and Antony, I perch precariously on top of a stack of chairs and give my cousin a nervous wave from afar. He grins at me and cocks his hat, a black fedora.

That's right, a fedora. And I do not know how to feel about it. I've never seen Antony wear anything to draw attention to himself. That's more Madi's bag. She loves wearing all one colour. And I mean *everything* in one colour, from underwear to hair ribbon. But she's nine, and you can get away with that kind of freakery at nine. For now, the jury is still out on whether Ant can get away with that hat. I'm erring towards no.

I pull my knees up to my chest and play with an ink spot on my jeans. I'm loving this new no-uniform thing. Back in Canberra we had to wear these green dresses and jumpers. It gets worse. We had to wear them with brown shoes and brown socks or stockings. Gross, right? We were too scared to stand in large groups in case we got mistaken for old-growth forests and bulldozed.

Here it's all wear whatever you like as long you're covered. And people do wear *whatever* they want. Antony's hat might be weird to me because I know him and he's never been the kind to draw attention, but in the grand scheme of this school's collective fashion repertoire, it's but a drop in the sartorial ocean of questionable. There's a kind of alt/indie thing going on here, and everyone seems kind of hell-bent on expressing their individuality—actually screaming it. So much so that it makes me feel like screaming back, "I get it! I get it! You're all so unique!" Only they're not. There are, like, five girls in my year level doing the retro nineties neon-purple hair thing. Kind of defeats the purpose, doesn't it?

Oh yeah, that reminds me. By this point in the story, you probably want some kind of mental picture of me, right? I hate reading books where you can't really tell what a character looks like because the author doesn't tell you anything. It's so annoying. Okay, so here are the basics:

My name is Zelda. That's my dad right there for you, eternally overextravagant (you should see how he dresses). He loves the twenties. Like, *loves* them. I'm named after the wife of the guy who wrote *The Great Gatsby*. Actually, she was a writer too, but not as many people know that. She was also a bit insane, but Dad says not to worry about that part. Anyway, I go by Zel because who wouldn't shorten a name like that?

Compared to the kids in this school, I'm pretty boring. I have blonde hair that's kind of wavy and thick. It's cut into a bob that hangs somewhere below my jaw and my shoulder. People always say it's weird that I'm blonde and Italian. That's because everyone's got it in their heads that we're all brunette and dark eyed. So not true. I'm actually only half-Italian, but the blonde definitely comes from Dad.

My eyes are brown and biggish. I have a mole on my cheek, and I'm lucky, because my skin's olive and never gets pimples (so far, anyway), and I tan quite dark in summer like all the Italian side of my family. I'm medium tall. Not skinny, but not fat either. I have my dad's broad shoulders and slightly thick legs (lucky me, right?). I had to get my first bra when I was eleven (awkward). I hate summer because I only like to wear boots. I pretty much live in jeans or jeans shorts, depending on the season. I'm not that girly, I guess, but I can't leave the house without mascara and eyeliner. What else? I have my ears pierced, but I always forget to wear earrings or I lose them. I hate wearing a watch. In fact, the only jewellery I wear are necklaces. I have this one chain, and I like to thread different things on it, depending on my mood. Basically, I'm pretty normal looking. Cute, but definitely no knockout. And given that I've spent a lot of my life around Mum's job, I consider myself a pretty good judge of looks.

As the bell rings for the start of Drama, the classroom door bangs open and closed, and the shortest man I have ever witnessed who is not an actual dwarf bounds into the middle of the room. "Hi, everyone. If we haven't already met, please call me Peter."

That's another thing about the school. The teachers don't mind the senior school kids calling them by first name.

He claps his hands together loudly, and I jump, nearly falling off my pile of chairs. "Okay, warm-ups! Most of you know the drill," he booms. "Up you get."

Apparently everyone does, because the entire class clambers to its feet and forms a circle. I join everyone, immediately terrified. Did I tell you that I'm horrible at doing stuff in front of audiences? Like, doing *anything* when I know someone is watching me? I get incredibly self-conscious—not to mention clumsy. Like, if you *want* an accident to happen, just give me a bowl of hot soup or coffee or something equally spillable and make me walk across the room in front of an audience. Someone's going to get hurt. It's most likely going to be me, but ask yourself, is that a risk you're willing to take?

So again I ask, why the hell did I ever think Drama was a good idea for a painfully awkward individual such as myself? Peter hasn't even told us what to do for warm-ups, and I can already feel myself turning bright pink.

What we end up doing is the weirdest, loudest, and longest game of Follow the Leader I've ever seen. At first, Peter is in front. "Okay!" He lets off another one of those firecracker claps, and I, of course, jump again. The lanky, pimpled guy next to me gives me a sympathetic but slightly patronising grin, like I'm the frightened noob I am. I ignore him and focus on what Peter is saying. "You've just woken up. Walk like you walk to the bathroom first thing in the morning!"

Okay, that's not too bad. That I can do. I affect a zombie shuffle and join in with the others, moving in this tight circle around a square metre of the available floor space. Some kids are quieter like me, just dragging their feet and feigning yawns. Some are more theatrical, groaning and swearing and stomping. Some act like they've woken up late. Of course, just when I'm thinking this isn't so bad, it starts to escalate. Peter keeps changing the game. First we're strutting angrily, and then we're being chickens and monkeys and little old ladies. Suddenly, there are lots of sounds involved. The room is getting louder and everyone's walking faster and my face is turning even redder. And then I have a horror-thought: if this is just warm-ups, what the hell is coming next? That's when Peter starts pulling different people out to lead the game. *Oh no, no, no*, I pray. Please spare me.

You can guess what happened next, right? Of course. Because this is why that Murphy guy came up with his law. I'm scampering past him, being a dog but trying to make myself three inches tall at the same time so he won't pick me, when he taps my arm.

"Right, you lead," he hollers over the cacophony of panting and barks.

The blood sprinting to my face seems to deprive my brain of all nourishment, because I can't think of a single thing to do. Everything I think of has already been done.

Next thing you know, I'm playing drunk. Which is weird enough, because I've never been drunk in my entire life. Never even been tipsy. (I'm kind of a good kid.) Still, I stagger around, acting like I've just knocked back six shots of whiskey. I can feel the class behind me doing the same. *This isn't so bad*, I think. Then Peter yells, "Change!" and again I'm stuck. Then I just throw on this walk. All cocky like I'm fabulous, channelling my prefect princess from the other school. The class follows suit. Then, thank God, it's someone else's turn.

Finally, the torture is over, and we stand in a circle and do some weird breathing exercises. Then everyone's back on the floor while Peter talks. I sit next to Antony this time, but he pays no attention to me. He's sitting cross-legged, back straight, all attentive like some little boy swot in primary school.

I can't blame him, really. Peter might not come up much higher than my shoulder, but this guy knows how to command a room. He's got this booming voice and this really...*present* energy. It kind of reminds me of some of the best girls at Mum's work. That's what makes them stand out, Mum told me. All the girls are stunning, of course, even the weird, gawky ones that only turn out beautiful in photos. But Mum says you can always tell which ones are going to do well by the way they carry themselves. They have confidence. Not cockiness, necessarily, which Mum hates, but a quiet kind of assurance. It's the kind of thing the clients love, apparently. I wonder what Prim will be like when she starts working. Prim's not exactly assured, but she's not nervous either. She just *is*. But Prim's an exception to a lot of rules.

I tune back in because Peter's talking about what we'll be doing this term. And people are actually listening, unlike in Biology, where the collective attention span lasted about seventeen minutes. Pretty sad for the first class of the year. Or normal, maybe. One minute we're getting a week-to-week rundown of the lab schedule, and the next there are iPhones peeking out under lab benches, scribbles filling up the margins of textbooks, and eyes fixed on the big blue sky out the window. Not me, though, because I'm kind of a geek.

While Peter talks, there's not a phone in sight. "Theatre," he booms, "did not just function as a form of entertainment for some playwrights. Many wrote with social or political purpose. There are playwrights whose work showed us an accurate and poignant glimpse of the political times, such as Chekov or Miller. Then there were those who were using theatre to transform their audience's views of their world, like the political satirists of early Athens, or Brecht."

I look around, and everyone's nodding. I chew my lip. Some of these names are vaguely familiar, but that's about it. I do like the idea of using art for political reasons, though. A lot of photographers we looked at in my class back in New York do that too. The worst part is that I'm not sure what this political theatre topic is going to mean for my doing-things-in-front-of–an-audience future. And you can probably imagine that if just warm-ups freak me out that much, this is very much on my mind.

"So this is what I expect of you for your major assessment this term," Peter goes on. "A piece of performance with a political or social commentary through it. Over the weeks, you'll be working in groups to devise a performance of some kind that addresses an issue. It will be based on a theme I'll give you next week. I don't mind what tradition of performing arts you work within, as long as it's appropriate to your mission." I wonder if it matters that I don't even know what he means by different traditions of performing arts. I better ask Antony that one later.

"The important thing is that you work to theme and that you offer some challenges or questions to your audience about the ideas you are working with." He holds up a hand. "Now, can I trust you to sort yourselves into groups, or do I have to do it for you?"

Obviously no one wants to be put into groups, because the room begins to heave and shuffle and mutter. Antony plucks at my sleeve. "Come on." He scrambles to his feet. I obediently follow him to the corner where a scratched wooden desk is wedged under a noticeboard. Seconds later we're joined by another girl and boy. She's kind of dramatic looking, with this long black hair piled on top of her head and thick-rimmed glasses that I can immediately tell are just for looks. She's short and kind of chunky, and her outfit is all draping skirt and woven scarf. The boy is tall and lanky, and his skin is a deep dark brown. Compared to the other kids, he's practically in formal attire, with his untorn jeans and an ironed green shirt buttoned nearly to the top. He kind of bounces a little as he stands there, like he's moving to some music only he can hear.

The minute we sit down, the girl rubs her hands together. "Finally. A project I can sink my teeth into."

"Here we go." The boy laughs and rolls his eyes but in a kind of teasing way.

"We need to come up with a killer idea," she says, ignoring him.

"We will." he says. "Be cool. We haven't even got our theme yet."

"It doesn't hurt to brainstorm a little," Antony tells him.

"Exactly," the girl says, giving Antony an approving nod.

I start to wonder what kind of rabidly earnest thespian types I've been thrown among. Should I be nervous? I decide the answer is no when the boy turns and gives me this wide, warm smile.

"Hi," he says. "Who are you?"

"I'm Zel. I'm his cousin." I jab Antony's arm. Kind of hard too. For not introducing me in the first place.

"Hi Zel, I'm Michael." He has a slight accent, but I can't pick it. It's like one of those faint accents kids get from their parents. But I'm too much of a geographical dunce to have a clue where it's from.

"Sorry," Antony mutters, rubbing his arm. "Everyone, this is Zel."

The girl peers over her glasses at me and nods. "I'm Ashani. Have you done drama before?"

I shake my head. She nods in this knowing way, and I get the feeling she's already thinking of me as some sort of barnacle attached uselessly to her great vision. Given that she's right, I don't bother being annoyed.

The three of them start reminiscing about some play they were all in last year. I tune out. Instead of listening, I do what I always do in these moments since we moved here: I figure out what time it is in New York and work out what I'd be doing if I were there. I check my phone. It's night-time now on a Sunday. I'd probably be coming home from a subway trip with Prim or maybe from the photography centre. Then, when I'd get home, Mum and Dad and I would go out for dinner. Dad's always had this thing about eating dinner out on Sunday. He says it makes the fact that it's Monday the next day more bearable. I always thought that was kind of strange because both Mum and Dad love their jobs. But I don't question it. I love our dumb tradition.

When I finally tune back into the conversation, the Drama nerds are still talking shop, and they only stop when the classroom door opens and a girl walks in. She hands a note to Peter, who nods and pockets it without looking at it. Both Ashani and Antony wave at her.

"Stell! Over here!" Ashani calls.

The girl gives them a hint of a nod and steps lightly between the clusters of kids on the ground. The first things I notice about her are her red hair, which is tied into a messy bun at the top of her head, and her immaculate posture. My grandmother, who's always telling me to straighten up (ha), would go gaga over her impeccably aligned shoulders and neck.

"Where were you?" Ashani asks as the girl drops down next to Ant.

"Ollie," she mumbles.

The others nod knowingly but say nothing.

"Zel, this is Stella," Antony mutters, remembering his manners this time.

Michael chuckles and slaps his thighs. "Zel and Stell!"

I ignore him and say hi. She kind of bares her teeth at me in that way that passes for a smile but isn't really one. Great, she seems about as friendly as Ashani. She doesn't join the conversation either. She doesn't even ask what we've been doing. While the others continue where they left off, she fixes her gaze to the middle distance, her arms wrapped around her waist. She's still got her backpack on her back too, as if she's prepared to bolt at any moment. I start to wonder how she became a part of this motley group.

She's so pale and so thin, it's almost like she's only just holding onto existence, to having a form. Her face is freckled, and her eyes a pale blue. They, too, seem barely there. Her cheekbones, as my mother would say, could cut diamonds. I'm trying to work out if I think she's pretty or not and have just decided that she probably is when she's not frowning when Peter does that hand clap/explosion thing. I wonder how long it will take until I don't jump half a metre every time he does that.

We spend the rest of the class doing what he calls "improv" where we're given scenarios and a minute to come up with an idea, then told to act them out. The others are really good. Ashani takes it really seriously, coming up with ideas and changing characters with quicksilver efficiency. She tries really hard, but it's Antony who is kind of amazing. Everyone else is clearly play-acting, but he's actually believable. Peter keeps praising him for his "commitment" to character, whatever that means. I watch him, wondering who this kid is who stole my doofy, shy cousin.

Just like warm-ups, I hate improv with every fibre of my being. I muddle through, mostly keeping to the background of scenes, playing trees and dead people. And I wonder if I can get through the whole term doing that.

CHAPTER 5

The first thing I do when I get home from school is check to see if Prim's online. She's not, of course. Even if she wasn't probably-maybe avoiding me, she's hardly ever online anyway. Prim's one of the few kids I know of our age who isn't hog-tied to the internet.

By the way, you should probably know that Prim would kill me if she knew I was telling you her name is Prim. She hates that name. Mostly because that drip of a little sister (her words) in *The Hunger Games* had it. Prim hated that character because she had to be looked after all the time. "She needed to grow some serious balls," she'd say. Prim hates the weak and the useless. Well, she hates them if they have a choice *not* to be. I think that's why I was so flattered when she liked me. I tried to explain to her once that Katniss needed something to protect to explain her motivation to even join the Hunger Games in the first place. That wasn't good enough for Prim. There's no convincing her when she believes something.

Prim's full name is Primulka. Suddenly Zelda doesn't look so strange, right?

My face scrunched with disbelief the first time she told me. "Primulka? What kind of name is that?"

"A batshit crazy one, like my mother."

It's true too. Both parts. At first, I assumed it was some exotic European name. Czech or Russian or something. But it turns out it's from nowhere. Prim's mum just made it up. Saw it written on a clothing label and liked the sound of it. And Prim's mum *is* kind of crazy. I never met her except the once, the day before I left, but Prim told me enough about her.

I never call her Primulka. I mean, who's got time to be saying all those consonants? And luckily, I seem to be the only person on earth who is allowed to call her Prim. If anyone else does, she gives them her best death stare.

"It's *Primulka*," she'll say in that haughty voice she reserves for those who've transgressed some precious Prim boundary. (There are a lot of those.) She does it even though she hates her full name as much as she hates the short version. But that's the drama of Prim for you.

"Why don't you change your name?" I asked her that day. "Models do it all the time."

"Too pretentious."

"Not if you call yourself Lisa or Pam or something totally regular."

That made her smile, which made me happy. Because even though I'd only just met her, I somehow knew I was getting a rare treat.

Anyway, Prim didn't change her name. She remains Primulka to the rest of the world because she's a stubborn idiot and her mother is nuts. And to me, she's Prim. Prim the Impossible. Prim the Mighty. Prim the Beautiful.

Prim who is not online. Ever.

I clunk downstairs and wander into the sunroom. Dad's at his desk, sketching at a design.

"Zelda," he bellows when he sees me, and he immediately stops what he's doing. That's what Dad's like. He's always busy, but never is for Mum and me. Okay, you might have to brace yourself for this next bit of information: I *like* my parents. I don't mean I love them because they're my mum and dad and I'm stuck with them. I mean I really, really like them. I like hanging out with them. I like talking to them. I like doing stuff with them. They're super busy, but Mum and I always eat breakfast together, Dad and I always hang out, and our Sunday dinner is an institution that shall not be violated for any other social plan but births, weddings, or funerals.

I have this vision of being older and maybe married with kids, even (if the government ever lets us, of course), and I'll still be joining them for Sunday dinners. I know this is not normal for most sixteen-year-olds—the ones I know, anyway—but it's just how it is. Maybe it's because it's always just been the three of us. No sibling tension to complicate things.

"So, how was the hippie school?" Dad's got it in his head that the new school is more like a commune than an actual school.

I sprawl on the couch in the corner and pluck at Mum's new plant. "Yeah, it was kinda hippie." It wasn't really, but it was definitely looser than any other school I've been to.

He chuckles. "I'm still stunned Rosa let Antony go to that place."

"Me too. You should have seen him in Drama class, though. Boy's got moves."

"Drama? What are you, the self-proclaimed queen of awkward, doing in a drama class?"

I pull a leaf from the plant and tear it up into tiny pieces. "No French. How was the theatre today?"

"Great," he says with gusto.

Did I tell you my dad's a costume designer? His grandparents were both costumiers in Italy. When they came out to Australia in the sixties, my grandad opened a costume shop in Canberra. It was the only one for a long time, so they were really busy and successful. Dad learned everything from them. They wanted him to run the shop when they retired, but he didn't want to. He just wanted to design clothes for stage and to learn fancy beadwork, which looks as fiddly and boring as it sounds. Dad loves it, though.

That's what he did in New York while Mum worked at the agency. A friend of his got him some work at an opera company. He must have impressed them, because that's what landed him the one-year contract with this company in Sydney. See what I mean about my high-achieving parents? I wish they'd stop impressing people so we could stop moving.

I guess working for the theatre is just another thing that sounds kind of glamorous but isn't, really. Dad said he spent most of his days in New York in a tiny room under the stage with a coven of little old nonnas bickering and beading. It was just like his childhood, he would joke.

And for me, it wasn't so great either. Because we got free opera tickets. Imagine my joy about that. If you can't, imagine having to sit through two hours of people wailing in another language just because your dad designed some beads on a vest. My appendix burst when I was eleven and it was less painful.

If you looked at my dad, you probably wouldn't be surprised he's into costumes. He's not afraid of a loud shirt (like *really* not afraid) or a crazy tie pattern. And he's also got kind of big hair. That's because it's super curly. I used to get embarrassed because people always looked at him.

Prim used to say if she saw my dad on the street, she'd swear he was gay. I told Dad that, and he just laughed. He said people used to always assume he was when he was younger too because he wore bright colours and wanted to work in the theatre. But Dad actually really likes boobs. Which is lucky for my mum, because she has them. *Ew.* Did I just talk about my mum's boobs? Gross. Pretend I said nothing. *Anyway,* Dad always says he doesn't care if people assume he's gay, because it's not an insult. And I know that he says that for me. Another reason why I love my dad.

Mum and Dad met at a nightclub when Mum was twenty. It was the late eighties, and they had this matching giant hair. (Mum's was the product of a good half hour with a hairspray can, though, she says.) I've seen the photos. It was epic. They've been together ever since. They are kind of disgustingly in love still. Not like Rosa and Uncle Antonio. Rosa used to always say, "I love him, but I'm sick to death of him." I wonder if she wishes she hadn't said that now. Mum would never say that about Dad. They never seem to get tired of each other, and they don't ever fight. They argue, but they don't fight. Maybe that's why they waited ages to have me.

Prim said her mum and dad didn't talk to each other for five months before he finally moved out. Like, not a single word. They lived in the same apartment and didn't even make eye contact. For the last two months, her mother slept on a couch in Prim's room. That's when Prim told them they had to sort it out or one of them had to get out. I don't know if Prim thought it would actually happen, that she'd end up moving to Brooklyn with her mother. I get the feeling she didn't. But it's hard to know what Prim feels sometimes. And it's even harder to get her to talk about it. Which is probably pretty obvious from the radio silence I'm currently experiencing, right?

Dad pushes up his glasses, rolls up his pink (see?) shirtsleeves, and peers at me over his pencil. "You doing okay?"

And I know he's asking about Prim. I never told Dad anything about us, exactly, but I know he's guessed, because of the tone he gets in his voice when he asks about her. I don't really know why I don't tell them. Maybe it's just because I'm not even sure what there is to know. And I don't think talking about it will make it any less confusing. The only thing that will is if Prim speaks. And that's not looking like it's happening anytime soon.

So, in the tradition of teenage communicativeness, I just shrug and say, Antony style, "I'm fine."

"Did you meet any good people at the school?"

"I met some of Antony's friends. They were okay, I guess. And a guy called Jason in Art class. He seemed kind of cool."

He was. Kind of chill and surfer-ish and into photography like I am. He showed me his major project from last year. He takes stunning shots of the ocean. Not pretty landscapes or anything boring like that. Close-ups of water in motion. Waves about to break, swirling, kelpy whirlpools in muted grey greens. Kind of amazing.

I hardly met anyone else, really. But that's more my fault than theirs. People were pretty friendly, especially compared to when I first started school in New York. It was really hard to get to know people there at first. Kids were polite, pleasant even, and some of them got a kick out of meeting an Aussie for a minute. I was great as a novelty, I guess, because people chatted to me and asked me questions about Australia. But that was it. It felt like everyone already had their friendship groups and didn't need this random interloper with what was (apparently) a tricky accent tagging along.

The only people at school who bothered being friends with me were Beth and Keeley. But even then, I was just kind of their third wheel. It was pretty depressing. I was used to having a lot of friends back in Canberra. Another reason why I was glad to meet Prim when I finally did.

~ ~ ~

Later, after Mum gets home, we eat dinner out on the deck. It's just chicken and salad wraps, a team effort in lazy food prep. It's not an unusual dinner for us either.

It's one of those soft, windless nights where the air is laced with the scent of cut grass and feels super soft on your skin. I'm busy zoning, half listening while Mum and Dad natter about their days. Mum's talking about how her old hairdresser back in Canberra keeps emailing photos of her daughter. The woman's totally convinced the kid could be a model. This happens to Mum all the time. She's pretty good at letting them down gently, but this lady's pretty insistent.

Mum sighs and kicks her bare feet up onto the side of my chair. "I think I'm going to be getting a daily update on the child for the rest of my life. She's a pretty little thing, but she's about five foot tall. I swear," she mutters through a mouthful of wrap, "sometimes I'm tempted to send these women some of our girls' cards. Then maybe they'd get the picture."

"Or you run the risk of them becoming even more deluded, thinking their precious daughter would fit right in," Dad offers.

Mum nods slowly, looking resigned to her lot as the destroyer of dreams. Then she suddenly perks up. "Zel, did Primulka tell you her mum has let her sign on in time for Fashion Week?"

I jump at the sound of Prim's name, my eyes fixed on the bright-crimson bougainvillea blooms climbing the back fence. "Wow," is all I say, which is vague enough to mean I do know or I don't know. I don't think Mum has figured out that I haven't spoken to Prim for a while.

"I think she's going to do very well, that child. If she can hold on the attitude."

If she can hold the attitude. I have to smile. That's a big *if*. Manners aren't really Prim's strong suit. I mean, she says please and thank you and everything, but she just can't help saying what she thinks. And most people probably don't want to hear what Prim actually thinks.

I know I'm making Prim sound awful, but seriously, she's not that bad. She's just kind of a jagged person. And honest to a fault sometimes. And sure, there are a lot of people she doesn't like, but that's just because she's selective in who she gives a crap about. And that list is longer than you might think when you first meet her. First there are her older brothers. She says they're idiots, but I know she loves them. Then there's her cat, Violet. "My soul mate," Prim said when she introduced us. I nearly freaked at that. Mostly because it's the closest I've been to seeing Prim go squishy about anything *ever*. And it was also vaguely terrifying that she considered Violet—a skinny, smoky-grey thing—her soul mate, because that cat is evil. Like pure, true, call-on-a-medium-to-cleanse-the-spirits-from-any-place-that-cat-has-slept evil.

There's also her mum (maybe only because she has to, though) but definitely *not* her dad on the list. There's my mum. (I sometimes think she likes my mum better than she likes her own.) Prim actually laughs at Mum's jokes, which are usually deeply unfunny. Then the rest of the list is rounded out by the ancient sisters who run the laundry where she works, old people in general, cats, squirrels, and the Brontë sisters (how quaint of her, right?). Oh, and obviously, I'm on the list. High up there, but definitely lower than the cat. Well, I *was* high. Not so sure now.

"You're the only person my age that I like," she told me once.

It's not surprising she's doing Fashion Week. Prim is beautiful. Seriously beautiful. Not wholesome, girly pretty. Not sex-kitten hot. She's model beautiful. That skinny, gawky, "oops I'm not supposed to be stunning but I just happened to turn out like that" type.

She's got these fierce, dark brown eyes, her mum's dark hair, and her dad's super-pale Irish skin. (Well, she told me that. I've never even seen a picture of her dad.) She's kind of textbook model stuff, Mum says. Symmetrical but unique at the same time, with her long face and thin mouth. It shouldn't work, but it does.

Mum says Patrick, one of the agency's bookers, found her right there in New York while out getting everyone coffees. He came back looking like the cat that got the cream and stayed that way all day. Prim was only fourteen then, and her mum wouldn't let her sign anything until she thought she was old enough. I guess that time has finally come if she's doing Fashion Week.

In case you think I am deeply shallow, it wasn't Prim's looks that got me. Think about it. My mum works in a modelling agency. I practically grew up in one. I'm kind of used to models. Sure, they're all beautiful on the outside, but believe me when I tell you their insides are all different.

"Of course, she might not get many shows this year," Mum says, dragging me back to Prim's new brilliant career. "But you never know. It'll be a good experience for her."

I just nod as I pass Dad my empty plate, because it's hard to imagine Prim going into this new life without me there to watch.

CHAPTER 6

The Art teacher is incredibly serious. For starters, she's one of the only teachers who hasn't coughed up her first name for us to use, and this is our second class. In fact, she didn't even bother asking our names either. She just launched straight into the art talk. Her name is Stedman, but a few of the kids who seem to know her well call her "Mrs S". I don't call her anything, mostly because I haven't really spoken to her yet.

That's about to change, because she's coming around to each table, asking about our ideas for our major assignment. That was the summer homework, apparently, to have brainstormed ideas for our independent art projects. Of course, I only got the memo a week ago when we decided I would come here, so I'm hoping she'll go easy on the fact that my idea is basically a bunch of undeveloped films in a plastic container in my fridge at home.

Surfer-dude Jason is sitting next to me again, and he's already told me he's continuing with his water theme. He wants to work with film this time.

And when Stedman gets to him, she likes his idea immediately. I can tell by the thoughtful way she taps her fingernail on the table as she watches some of the videos he's already made. She's got this steel-grey hair that she wears in an immaculate bob, and she wears drapey tops and dresses in earthy browns and greens. She's also kind of still. She's the complete opposite of Leo, my teacher back in New York, who always wore a suit and tie and darted around like an excited kid. He's the one who taught me to use and develop real film, like they used to before what he called "the digital apocalypse" of cameras and smart phones. He was ancient and hilarious, and everything we did excited him.

I get the feeling this teacher won't be as easily impressed. She's all about "concept". She says the concept is as important as the art we produce, that this is what makes its existence worthy. Trouble is, I don't have a concept. I just have the photos from the subway project.

Stedman turns to me, and my guts immediately begin to clench. She leans her hip against the table and gives me a benign smile. "I don't think we've met before. You are?"

"Zel," I mumble. "I just came."

"Welcome," she says perfunctorily. "Have you got anything for me?"

"Um, not much."

Her lip thins out a little, so I quickly launch into a description of the subway project. When I'm done, she just kind of nods, one eyebrow cocked.

"So these photos are all taken?"

I nod, swallowing hard. "But not sorted or developed. They're, uh, still on the rolls." I don't tell her how abruptly it stopped. How the Coney Island pictures are still sitting on a half-finished film in my camera.

"Right." She taps her fingernail on the table. But only once, and I'm thinking this is not a good thing. "Well, you could certainly spend the term developing and organising the photos. And the project has a roundness to it I like. But I want to see you drawing on a conceptual basis for the selection of the pictures. While the project itself is interesting, it's not yet significant." She says the word *significant* significantly, if you know what I mean. "Have you got any ideas?"

Why does she make me so nervous? I decide it's those death ray eyes. "Uh, not really." Not a single clue, more like it.

"Well, that's your task for now. Talk to me next week." She gives me a smile, quick and cool, like she doesn't have time for smiles but knows she ought to. It kind of reminds me of Stella, the late girl from Drama class. "Nice to meet you, Zel."

And she's off to torment someone else. I let out a relieved groan.

Jason grins. "Terrifying, isn't she?"

"And *how*."

He chuckles. That's why I like Jason. He really is the kind of guy who actually chuckles. He doesn't smirk like most self-conscious teen guys who are too cool to just find something funny. A guy who chuckles is the kind of guy I can stand sitting next to in class all term.

He leans closer to his screen as he crops an image of rocks being battered by waves. "She's an incredible teacher, though. The terrifying is worth it, you'll see."

I just nod and stare at my blank page. I really hope so.

~ ~ ~

That night I take the container of films out of the fridge. I carefully open it up and count the rolls, like I don't already know how many there should be. Sixteen. And the one unfinished one in my camera. Nearly every trip we took, documented by at least a few photos and stored here in these little time capsules.

The subway project was Prim's idea.

It started with a book. Her favourite book in the world.

The book is how we met. I'd been in New York for a few months by that point. I was hunkered down in Mum's office, waiting for her to do a few things before we'd meet Dad for dinner. I sat on one of the couches where the girls wait for appointments, my homework in my lap. When Prim marched into the office, she waved at Mum, who was on the phone as usual, and flopped down on the couch opposite mine. She immediately pulled a book out of her bag and began to read.

I didn't pay much attention to her at first. I was doing some impossible quadratic equation thing. I hate maths—or math as they call it over there—and it takes every ounce of my concentration to do it. And like I said, I'm so used to the oversupply of beautiful girls wandering around, it didn't even occur to me to look up.

In fact, I usually deliberately ignore them. Mostly because the models who don't know me tend to stare. Being of only average human looks, height, and build, it's me—not they, the freakishly beautiful—who stands out like a sore thumb in this place. So they sit there and try to pretend they're not surreptitiously stealing looks at me, but they totally are. And I know it's because they're trying to work out what I'm doing here, when I am *clearly* not the talent. I can practically hear their brains whirring. Maybe I'm a secretary taking a break on the couch? Maybe I'm a new plus-size (read: normal girl size) model? Maybe I got lost, and I'm waiting for my mum to come get me?

The first time I realised what this stare-bear phenomenon was possibly about, I decided to test it. This wide-eyed blonde kept gawking. Over it and curious, I looked up and called out, "Hey, Mum?" Then I asked her some random, stupid question. The minute the girl connected, she stopped staring and opened a magazine.

But I didn't have to do that with Prim. She paid no attention to me at all. She just sat there and quietly read her book, gnawing on a fingernail. I think the fact that she wasn't paying any attention was what made me look up at *her*.

The first thing I noticed, of course, is how beautiful she is, even with her eyebrows drawn together and that small scowl which I now know as Prim's reading face (less fierce than her regular non-specific scowl). The second thing I noticed was the book, a thick paperback, the pages all wrinkled and yellow and loose. There was something instantly familiar about its garish red, blue, and silver cover design. It took me a minute to realise I'd been staring at the very same book cover this morning in the window of a second hand book store by my school as I waited for my bus. It was in a display of books set in New York, obviously aimed at tourists. That copy was in much better condition, though.

I'd just figured out where I recognised it from when Prim lifted her eyes from her page. "Is there something you need?" she said in this total monotone. Deadpan and just a little ominous.

I didn't know yet that everything Prim said or did was delivered in monotone. Later, I understood how it all contributed to her carefully constructed air of disinterest. It was her way of never showing she was attached to a person, a moment, or a thing. But at this point, it was just plain terrifying.

"Uh, no," I stuttered, shaking my head. "It's just…that book."

"What about it?" Prim flapped the tattered cover impatiently and a page dropped out, floating over to land next to my foot.

I leaned down and picked it up. "I saw this book in a shop yesterday, that's all." I gave her an appeasing smile as I passed back the page, though I wasn't exactly sure what I was appeasing.

"Really?" She shoved the fallen page back inside the book. "Was it in better shape than this?"

"It was, actually."

That livened her up a teeny bit. "I want to get it. Where'd you see it?"

I couldn't remember the name of the shop, but I could tell her where it was. I jotted down the location on a corner of my exercise book, ripped it out and handed it to her.

Prim took the piece of paper and gave me a quick smile. "Thanks."

Maybe it's because Prim doesn't smile much that when she does, it feels like being presented with something. Maybe it's because her smile is so damn beautiful, even in half bloom. I don't really know. But a smiling Prim is kind of an earth-shattering thing. Take it from me. And maybe because of that smile, I wanted to keep her talking. "So, what's the book about?"

And even though I asked, I was still kind of surprised she answered, what with that whole nonchalant-bordering-on-hostile thing she had going on. She did raise an eyebrow, as if she doubted my interest, but then told me it was the third time she'd read it, which explained the tattered cover and serious case of page dandruff. The whole time, her expression was that of the same blank girl who had first confronted me. But her eyes were dancing, betraying her. They belonged to another girl who couldn't contain her enthusiasm for something. And I knew then, even though I'd barely taken in a word of her description, that I'd find that book and read it someday. Just to talk to her about it.

Yeah, yeah, I know exactly what you're thinking. And yes, there was probably a crush in the making already if I was planning to wade through some tome with an ugly cover just because it made a beautiful, slightly scary girl betray her own aloofness. Of course I was crushing on her in that vague, fleeting way I do with any sassy, cute girl I meet. Because if there's one thing I've learned about myself is that I like difficult girls. And Prim was clearly capital-D difficult.

But the actual conscious crush? That part took a while. At this moment, she was just this fierce, intriguing girl who really liked a book. In fact, I didn't really think about her again until the next week when I was standing at the bus stop outside the bookshop again. I immediately looked for the garish cover. But the display of New York books was gone. I crossed my fingers for her sake that she'd found it.

And she must have. Because a week later, Mum came into my room after work and dropped something on my desk. "For you, from Primulka."

I just frowned, because I hadn't learned Prim's name yet, so I couldn't connect the girl I'd met to the brown paper bag on my desk. Then, when I opened the bag and saw the book, I grinned. What a fabulous weirdo. It was her old copy, even worse off than it had been before her last read. The cover looked ready to disintegrate, and fallen pages had been pushed back between others at haphazard angles. It was enough to give a librarian a heart attack. At least I wouldn't have to worry about dog-earing the pages.

That night I carefully taped them all back into the book and placed some contact over the cover. Then the next day at lunchtime, I actually started to read it. I knew straight away why Primulka—if that really was her name—loved the book. It was this funny, nostalgic story about these three people who move to New York City after they finish college. They all work dead-end jobs to support their art and live in a crappy apartment together, trying to figure out how to live the high life with their crazy bunch of New York friends with no money. One is an actor, one a poet, and one an artist. The actor has this epic unrequited crush on the poet that lasts their whole New York lives.

It was the first thing I read that made me want to get to know this behemoth of a city. It was this book that turned the city into this vibrant, alive thing that I wanted to explore. Only I didn't really know where to start.

It took me a week to read its four hundred pages. But it was also completely addictive, and I couldn't have stopped if I'd wanted to. I needed to know if the narrator would make it as an actor, and if he and the poet would get together. I needed to know if they'd ever get to Far Rockaway.

By Sunday night, all my questions were answered.

When I was done with it, I placed the repaired copy back into a brown paper bag and scribbled a little note onto it. *Thank you! I fixed it, in case you need to lend it out to anyone else.*

And I gave it to Mum to return to her, not sure if I'd see her again.

CHAPTER 7

Monday in Drama class, Peter gives us our theme for the group project. Home. At first I'm like *what*? Then the idea grows on me. Mostly because we spend the first half of class discussing all the ways home has meaning. All the things it can stand for, like safety, security, family, and love.

I don't talk much, but I listen. And after another weekend of nothing but me, the house, and my homesick heart, it feels pretty good just to be in a room with a crowd of people making noise and chatting and just being. It was a depressing weekend, raining from Friday morning until sometime Sunday night, as if the weather didn't want Sydney to have a weekend. And it was serious rain too, huge, heavy downpours that soaked you through within seconds of being outside. Antony told me this morning this is how Sydney does wet weather. There's nothing but sunshine for a month or two, and then it just pours for days. "Like a giant tantrum," he told me cheerfully. "Then we go back to sunshine."

I kind of liked the drama of it all. I like weather. And Sydney's full of it. Controlled by it. New York is so dominating it shapes the weather. In summer, the buildings throw the sun's heat, magnified, back at you. In fall, the streets make tunnels, taking light winds and turning them into freezing gales, turning the air brittle and more violent than it already is. In winter, the sea of buildings stop flurries from flurrying, as they melt against stone and steel before they have a chance of landing. Shop awnings catch melting snow and make icicles of it. But here in Sydney, the weather is so elemental it doesn't let something like a city get in its way.

Okay, I know some of you must be thinking, *shut up about New York, already. Shut up with the constant comparisons.* But I can't. Because this is what it feels like when you're strung between two places, between two lives. Maybe I'll forget New York soon. Maybe I'll be fully here one day. But right now, I'm still somewhere in between. You try being forced to move from the place you've lived all your life and having to get used to a new one. Then imagine the minute you get used to it—start to love it, even—you're told you have to move again. It's hard. Seriously, my parents are lucky I don't do delinquency, because this upheaval stuff sure could have sent me off the rails.

And maybe it's because I've had to suddenly move from what I'd considered home a couple of times in the last year that this talk in Drama class about home is interesting. Because it turns out there are a lot of kids here whose experience of home is connected with upheaval. One girl said for the last year since her parents divorced, she has lived her weeks divided exactly, down to the hour, between her parents' new homes. And it's so unsettling that she can't think of either place as home. Ashani says her grandmother still refers to where she lived in North India as home, like she is just visiting here, even though she has been in Australia for twenty-five years. She didn't even fully unpack for the first year, her grandpa says. Michael tells us how his parents always remind him about when they first moved to Sydney from Melbourne when he was seven and how, for a month, he kept asking when they were going home. He just couldn't understand that the new house was theirs. His mum said he was less confused than when they moved from Somalia a few years before that. "I was kind of dumb when I was a kid." He laughs and shrugs.

"When you were a kid?" some girl jokes.

Peter tells us about the writer, Nabokov, who wrote in his autobiography about the grief of his home completely disappearing while he was in exile. He could never fathom that the place he loved as a child had simply ceased to exist altogether. I can't even imagine that, but I get it. I say Canberra is dull, but I'd hate it if I could never go back. Or if I could never go back to New York or to Prim. If all those places we went together were just images on my camera, something I never got to experience. Heartbreak city.

When I think about it, I still consider Canberra to be home. That's where I felt most anchored. I lived in the same house for fifteen years. My nonna lived ten minutes' walk away. My cousins lived in the next street. I knew the grid around my house in that way you do when you're a kid and your small world is a universe. We knew every tiny thing—the puddle that never drained from the empty lot that was our own personal endless sea, the small patch of scrub down by the train tracks that became our jungle. Later, there was the half-built house that became our own, its rooms furnished with our imaginations. And when I was older, I'd hang out with my friends there, a place where we could compare life notes on this thing called puberty away from our parents' ears. All that was home. Until it wasn't any more.

Peter claps his hands to signify the end of our discussion. This time I only flinch. And now it's time for the horror show that is improv games. Just as we're getting started on this stupid one called Space Jump, Stella, the late girl from last week, turns up. She doesn't even show Peter a note this time. She scurries over to sit down next to Ashani, pushing a few stray hairs up into her topknot. I wonder what's up with her. Does she just like an extra-long lunch? She's lucky it's Peter. I get the feeling if it were one of the other teachers, there'd be a lot more caring about it.

I get through Space Jump using last week's MO, playing inanimate objects or animals. I see Peter eyeing me at one point, so I'm not sure how long I'll get away with it. When the bell finally rings, I make a break for the door, but Ashani grabs my sleeve and yanks me towards the others.

She prods her glasses (which I'm still positive are fake; there's, like, no magnification) up her nose, looking *très* businesslike. "Right, we need a meet-up to work on ideas."

Antony and Michael nod vigorously. Stella lifts her eyes in the briefest suggestion of an eye roll. I smile. I guess I'm not the only one who thinks this girl is walking a thin line between (self-appointed) team leader and dictator. Ashani whips out her phone and turns to me. "Right, first we need to get your details, so we can all communicate."

"We could just start a Facebook group," I suggest.

Ashani's shudder is highly exaggerated. "I don't *do* Facebook."

Stella gives me a sliver of a smile. I have no idea if she's smirking at me or Ashani, but I shoot her a look just in case. She stares at me blankly for a second and looks away.

"I think we should meet after school one day." Ashani checks the calendar on her phone. I raise an eyebrow. I can't imagine ever having enough of a life here that I'd need to check my calendar. "How's Tuesday?"

"We've got dance, remember?" Stella says, tapping her foot. What? She's eager to get to her next class? She only just made this one.

Ashani's face falls. "Oh yeah. We could meet after that, I guess." She points at me. "If we tell her where it is."

Her? She's forgotten my name? *Seriously*? I give her a look. "One, my name is Zel. Two, you all dance?" I seriously hope this isn't anything to do with Drama. Because you know the level of suck with me and Drama? Times it by about five hundred, and that's me dancing.

"Me and Ant and Stella do," Michael says.

I stare at Antony. "You?"

He shrugs. "It's good for actors to learn movement."

"We started last year." Michael points to himself and Antony. "Stell's been doing it for ages, though."

That explains the skinny and the eternal bun, then. But before I can even conjure an image of Antony doing modern dance, Ashani butts in again. "Okay, can everyone do Wednesday after school?"

I know for a fact I am free. For the rest of my life, apparently. I nod. The boys do too. Then everyone turns to look at Stella. She shrugs and chews her lip. "Maybe."

They just nod and start to discuss time and place stuff. I am *so* confused. They seem so gung-ho, yet they don't seem to care at all about Stella's total lack of interest or commitment. It's weird. I get the feeling that if it were me or the boys, Ashani would be seriously kicking ass over the attitude.

"Okay, the cafe at four on Wednesday." Ashani shoves a pen through her bun and turns for the door. "See you later."

Like a pubescent minion army of two, the boys scurry to follow her. I trail them slowly, watching as Stella falls into step behind them, part of the group but not really.

~ ~ ~

I bounce my toe up and down on the crossbar of the table and eye Mrs Stedman. Next to me, Jason sketches the cardboard box at the front of the room. That's what we're supposed to be doing. Instead, I continue my visual stalk of the teacher. She's still halfway across the room, talking to this tizzy girl, Tara.

I'm in Lit class with Tara. She talks to me sometimes, but she's one of those girls whose way of talking is to just fire questions at you, as if she's just trying to gather enough intel, assessing your cred against hers. What she doesn't realise is that I feel sorry for her. It must be exhausting to care that much. I'm perfectly happy with my middle-ranking social lot in life. Besides, being cool at this school looks like way too much hard work. I'd have to get up an hour earlier just to work on that effortlessly casual boho look.

Jason and I are at what has become our private table, a small one cornered by the window and the storeroom. It's quieter here away from the kids at the long tables who've enrolled in art as a bludge subject. They just sit there and yap all class, putting Instagram-level filters on their iPhone snaps in Photoshop or making collages out of magazines and calling it art. Don't get me wrong, I actually like Instagram. I just don't think putting a filter on a picture of yourself or a sunset is that interesting. I guess I'm one of those Insta snobs. I only follow actual photographers, and I won't put one of my own photos up unless I think it's perfect. This means I post once in a blue moon. No food art, and no selfies allowed either.

Here in our corner, Jason and I have peace and quiet and a view through the gum trees out to the football field. We're good deskmates. We both love Art class, and he says we balance each other artwise, too. We're both into photography, but he's all mister-quick-fingers Apple boy, doing everything on Adobe suites.

My foot starts bouncing again when I notice Stedman has moved from Tiff to the guy next to her.

Jason presses his hands to the table. "Relax, dude. They're going to be able to measure this on the Richter scale soon."

"Sorry," I mumble and stop. "What am I going to do? I've got nothing."

He makes a ticking sound with his tongue and shakes his head. "You're in *big trouble*," he sings.

"Don't! Don't even joke!" I practically squeal. God, what's happening to me? Fear has turned me into a high-pitched girlie girl. Jason just laughs.

I still don't have a concept. Not one I think Stedman's going to like, anyway. It's not that I didn't think about it either. I'm too much of a girly swot not to have agonised over it all through Sunday and last night. But everything I came up with was so half-baked that even the slap-a-filter-on-it crew in the middle of the room wouldn't buy it as art.

My box of film from the subway project is all at school now. I started developing them this week. I didn't know where to start at first. I debated just randomly picking one, but for some reason, the potluck concept made me nervous. I didn't know what part of Prim and I would be uncovered. So I decided to start at the start.

Now I have the contact sheet with a bunch of the images lying on the desk in front of me, but I'm too freaked to even look at them until this ordeal is over. *Finally* Stedman drifts over to me. I automatically cover the contact sheet with my arm. I'm not ready for her to scrutinise that yet. It's bad enough her staring into my conceptless soul. She stares at Jason's sketch for a long moment but says nothing, in that scary way of hers. Then she turns to me.

"Zelda, how are you coming along with the concept for your subway photos?"

I can feel Jason's eyes on me, giving me a *you're kidding me, that's your name?* look. I studiously ignore him. "Uh, okay," I lie.

She leans a hip against the edge of the table and folds her arms. "Shoot."

Jason, sweet boy he is, discreetly melts away, letting me have this humiliation on my own.

"I guess I was thinking maybe it could be about how it's kind of unfinished. You know, the idea of the unfinished project," I stutter.

She drops her arms and drums a finger on the table surface, so I know she's about as enchanted with that idea as I am. "That's hardly a concept. That's really just a state of affairs, isn't it?" And when I just nod and don't contribute anything else, she goes on. "Ask yourself, how do your pictures tell us that story? Or, why is that story worth telling from the pictures?"

"Maybe it could be about how if you really take the time to explore a place, the more layers you find?" It's weak, and I know it.

She tips her head to one side, eyes narrowing. I don't know if that's a better or worse sign than the finger tapping. "Hmm, sounds a bit travel guide-ish. Kind of thin." She frowns again. "Keep thinking."

I let out a breath. It's not from relief, though. It's not like I'm any closer to figuring this out. It just sounds like she's handing me yet another Get out of Jail Free card.

She smiles, like she knows. *Of course* she knows. I'm starting to think she's all-powerful. "It's okay, Zel. You have time. You just need to find the thing that's going to pull it all together. Give these pictures a reason to be looked at other than for their own sake. Some photographers come in with a concept first, and that determines the pictures they'll take. Others focus on a series of things or people, like you did, and then use the resulting pictures to illustrate or make sense of something. That's what you need to do. You need to make conceptual sense of these photos."

I nod again, only half following her. I wish I was back in the States. Leo just looked at each individual photo on its own merits. He didn't demand they be part of some great big high-concept theory.

She taps the contact sheet, which I guess I haven't done as great a job concealing as I thought. "Just keep looking at the pictures and think about what they or the project might be telling you about your world."

She walks away. Letting out a breath, I stare down at the contact sheet. I like the idea of photos telling us something about the world. I do. I just have no idea what these are telling me. All I know is that they better. And soon.

CHAPTER 8

After the day of the book, I didn't see Prim again for months. She was never around when I was at the agency. I didn't know then that she wasn't properly a model yet, that the agency was waiting for her mother to say she was old enough to start. They kept in regular contact with her, though, getting her to come in from time to time, preparing her. Mum says they do that with promising girls to make sure they do turn up when it *is* time. I guess Prim was promising.

So it was lucky I even ran into her again. I walked into the office after school one day, and there she was, sitting on the edge of the desk next to Mum, her skinny-jeaned legs hanging down, punctuated by a pair of chunky black Docs. She scowled at something Mum was showing her and said something I couldn't hear. Whatever it was, it made Mum laugh.

I was sitting on one of the couches, waiting for Mum to be done, when Prim suddenly dropped violently on the couch next to me, huffing loudly and giving me this combo withering eye roll headshake thing, like I'd just seen her yesterday. She waved the picture of herself in her hand. "Modelling is so, so dumb. I mean, who stands like that?"

I peered at the photo. It was a typical full-body model shot. She was staring down the camera, all frown-mouthed and thick-browed, wearing black jeans and a tight tee. She looked just like a model. Beautiful and perennially somewhere between helpless and pissed off. Her hands were on her hips, her elbows akimbo, her head tipped to one side.

"Maybe in a yoga class?" I suggested.

Prim let out a little snort which might or might not have been a laugh and shoved the photo back into a folder in her knapsack. "Every job I get I'm going to have to remind myself that this profound stupidity is what will make me the big bucks—someday, anyway."

I laughed. Most of Mum's girls that had just started were all starry-eyed about it with big Milan dreams. Starry-eyed, Prim was *not*.

She sat back on the couch, crossing her legs, clearly not giving a crap that she had her mutinous boots on their nice plush lounge. She had way more important things to think about, it turned out. "So, you actually read it?"

I nodded, smiling. "Of course. It was awesome."

She nodded slowly as if to say *of course it was*.

We chatted about it for a while, talking about our favourite bits, trying to decide if the poet was crazy or actually just saner than everyone else.

Then we got talking about the subway part. At one point in the story, when the characters are young and broke and living through a scorching summer in New York City, they realise they can keep cool by finding air-conditioned subway cars and riding them all day. Somehow, this grows into a lifelong project where they try to ride every subway line to the end.

"I always wanted to do that," Prim said, scratching at a jagged edge of a green-painted fingernail. "Ride all the lines."

"It would be pretty cool." I'd barely gone anywhere beyond Manhattan. The other boroughs seemed like foreign lands.

"Want to?"

It was that simple. A two-word question that made us what we are (or aren't) now. I hesitated in that moment, though. Not because I didn't want to. Not because I didn't want to do something with this weird, beautiful force of nature next to me. It was simply disbelief that she'd asked.

And before I could conjure an answer, she shrugged. "I mean, I'm going to do it, anyway."

And that was the first sign I ever got that Prim was anything less than super confident. Well, it wasn't confidence exactly. More like an acute, long-term case of not giving one single crap. (But that has to take some confidence, right?) It was that flicker of knee-jerk defensiveness, the first sign that rejection might actually mean something to her. She's so brittle and tough that you could easily imagine rejection being a non-existent concept to her. But that little pre-emptive *never mind* told me she did care, a little, even if I never once got her to admit it.

"I'll do it," I said, shrugging. The show of nonchalance was a great big lie, of course. I just felt like I was supposed to be playing her game.

Really, I was excited. My sort-of friends at the school, Keeley and Beth, would never do anything like this. They were more the group bake, study-buddy, bitch about boys ("We can talk about girls too if you want, Zel.") types. I joined in, but only because the kind of people who might have been more my type weren't exactly lining up to be best friends at my new school.

She immediately yanked a subway map from her bag and started straightening it out on her lap. I guessed we were doing it.

"Hey, maybe we should know each other's names, at least, before we get started?" I suggested, grinning.

She shrugged as if to say *if you really think it's necessary.*

That's when I found out her name was Primulka. And that was the end of the biographical detail sharing. At first I thought Prim didn't share that kind of stuff because she was really private. She is, I guess, about the really important stuff. But the other mundane get-to-know-you things—like street addresses, siblings, favourite bands and shows—that didn't come for a while. I think all that chitchat just bored her.

"Let's do the first line on Saturday afternoon," she said.

While I was mildly insulted that she just assumed I was free, she was right. I was nearly always free. And if by some miraculous chance I wasn't, I'd make myself free. Because this was potentially the most interesting thing that had threatened to happen since we moved to New York.

I stared at the map spread over her legs. I'd never really looked at a New York subway map before. There were so many lines. Where would we even start?

"We have to save Far Rockaway for last," she said. "Like in the book."

"How about Coney Island?" My finger traced a line that ran through Brooklyn. I still hadn't been there yet. And I liked the thought of starting with a well-known destination. I knew it would make my parents happier too when I told them about this.

Prim shook her head. "Too clichéd. Boring."

"Then you decide," I told her a little snippily.

"Okay." She shut her eyes, drew rapid little circles in the air over the map, and then jabbed her finger down somewhere in Queens. She opened her eyes again and peered at it. The closest line was purple. The 7 line. She traced it to the end with her finger and grinned. It looked like we were going to Main Street, Flushing, in Queens. The only thing I knew about Flushing was from re-runs of that old sitcom, *The Nanny*.

"Queens it is," I said, all confident, like I had any idea what that meant.

We agreed to meet at 34th and 5th at the Starbucks near the stop where our lines converged. Then Prim left me there on the couch, wondering what Mum and Dad would say about this plan.

When I finally did tell them about the project, they didn't say no. But they weren't exactly thrilled either. Mum felt a bit better than Dad because she knew Prim had been living here a couple of years and at least knew her way around the subway system. Dad muttered about it for a while but finally said, "Dear God, I can't say no. You're sixteen, and you have to start exploring the world by yourself. Be bloody careful!"

I grinned and jumped up to go get my phone to tell Prim I'd be there on Saturday. That's when I realised I didn't even have her phone number. I'd just have to turn up.

~ ~ ~

When I got to the Starbucks, Prim was already outside, clutching a coffee as big as her head. She was wrapped in a long khaki jacket and wearing her skinny black jeans and boots, with a grey scarf wrapped around her neck to her chin. And that was basically Prim's uniform. I liked it. I always like it when girly-looking girls dress like tomboys. It's cute.

"You getting something?" she asked as greeting.

I shook my head. I don't do coffee. I know that's practically un-Australian, but caffeine makes me crazy. Not in a good way. Besides, if I were caught at a Starbucks, my coffee-snob nation would probably revoke my citizenship.

"Let's go, then." She turned and clattered down the steps into the bowels of the subway before I could even finish shaking my head. I slipped my MetroCard out of my pocket and followed her, pulling my knapsack straps up onto my shoulders. I had my new camera stashed in there and was hyperaware of not losing it or breaking it.

It only took a minute for a train to arrive. It was packed, of course, full of Saturday trippers, weekend workers, and tourists. But the crowds thinned out after we crossed the East River, and we found seats in the middle of the car.

I remember that we didn't talk much on that first trip. It was too loud and busy. I just did what I usually do on the subway and watched people. In Australia, trains are kind of tame and boring. In New York, it felt like the subway was its own country, lawless, wild.

I always loved how it forced unlikely seat neighbours and encounters that would never happen any other way. Like the guy with the tattooed neck and the little old lady with the pink floral shopping bags who sat opposite us. Nowhere else would these people commingle but on public transport. I remember how they studiously ignored each other until she got up for her stop and dropped her umbrella. He picked it up and handed it to her without meeting her eye. That didn't stop her from thanking him and calling him "honey."

He pretended not to hear, but I could see the flicker of pleasure or embarrassment in the way he set his jaw, stopping a smile, and fixed his stare harder at the wall opposite. That's when I started filling in his backstory in my mind. I love doing that, weaving myself tales about people to pass the time. And I found out pretty quickly that Prim has exactly the same hobby, only slightly more extreme. In fact, she was at her morbid best on the subway.

My imaginings were suddenly ground to a halt by Prim's. She nudged me. "See that guy?"

I looked around me. Before I could get my sarcasm on and tell her there were a lot of guys on this train, she nudged me again harder. "The one in the blue shirt at the end. Don't you think he looks textbook serial killer?"

Even though I told her I was pretty sure there was no such thing as a textbook serial killer look, I looked anyway. And despite what I'd said, I saw what she meant straight away. At first glance, he looked pretty normal. But there was something slightly off about him too. His outfit, a pale blue shirt and grey trousers, were just a little bit too neat, too pressed. And then there was his skin, so pale it was kind of translucent. It made him look sickly. He had a sharp nose and long bony fingers that clutched the newspaper in front of him. Super tidy looking. Like he'd wash his clothes after every single wear and shower twice a day. He was exactly the guy they'd cast as a murderer in a film, because he's the guy-next-door type but ever so slightly creepy at the same time. "I totally see it."

"Who do you think he kills?" she asked me. "Kids or old ladies?"

"Neither." I told her, like I was some sort of expert profiler. "Young married couples," I said, for no reason other than it was the first thing that came to my mind. "Because it's more of a challenge," I improvised, "to get two at once. Especially when you lack physical strength. You have to be really clever."

Prim raised an eyebrow, looking vaguely impressed. This made me squee in a way that should have sent alarm bells ringing at this point. "So what's his weapon of choice?" she asked, clearly happy to surrender the narrative to me.

And that's how we mostly communicated. Through tales told to each other. We spent most train rides making up stories about everyone around us. Prim's stories were usually completely gruesome and awful. Mine, she claimed, were quietly insane. The scariest kind. I was happy with that.

I was about to start in on the chem lab he kept in his basement for drugging victims, wanting to impress her more, when we hit the last stop. She grabbed my wrist and yanked me out the door, not dropping my arm until we were bouncing down the platform. I remember how good it felt to have her skinny fingers wrapped around my wrist, her excitement palpable in that unexpected grasp.

That's another moment when I probably should have known I was working up a monster crush on Prim. I mean, I was already trying to impress her, wasn't I? Not to mention that she was beautiful and weird, two highly enjoyable things, as far as I'm concerned. But I didn't realise. I think I was more in worship mode. Here was this fierce, beautiful girl who did things like exploring every subway line because it happened in a book she loved. And she wanted to do it with me. I was still stuck on that.

CHAPTER 9

By Wednesday, hump day, Sydney's pretending the rain never happened. Antony and I amble down to the café where we're supposed to meet everyone, enjoying the sun on our faces. I'm feeling kind of mellow and good. Finishing up a double period of Psych that skirted uncomfortably close to maths will do that to a girl. Childhood mental development and mood disorders I can do. Statistics, I cannot.

Maybe it's because I'm so used to having no plans that I'd completely forgotten we were supposed to meet today for the Drama project. It wasn't until Antony collared me somewhere between the lockers and the front gate that I remembered.

We're meeting at a café not far from school where all the Year 12s come down and get lunch. No one else is allowed. According to school rules, we're not mentally or physically capable of walking four hundred metres down a street and handling real money to buy our lunch from strangers until we're in our final year. It's weird, because this school is so loose with the lack of uniforms and the calling teachers by their first names stuff. But becoming masters of our own lunchtime is apparently a step too far. Michael's got a theory that the rule's just there to keep the school canteen in business. That wouldn't surprise me. My advice to the earth mums who run that place is that if they stop trying to pretend kale crisps and honey-roasted pumpkin seeds are a worthy replacement for salt and vinegar chips and Mars bars, they'd do slightly better business.

"How was your day?" I ask Antony as we walk. Because if I don't get the conversation ball rolling, he won't talk. A fact of our lives. I remember the first time he came down to stay with Nonna in Canberra. We were five. As soon as his parents left, he wandered off into the backyard on his own. Even though my parents had sent me there especially and I was dying to play with this mysterious cousin from Sydney, I had to hunt him down in the backyard to play with him.

It's lucky I was a terrier of a kid, frankly. I wouldn't let go until he'd play hide-and-seek in the veggie patch with me. Otherwise we'd still be strangers. Antony's always danced to the beat of his own drum (literally now, apparently).

Which reminds me: "So, the dancing? Tell me about the dancing."

He shrugs. "It's good to surrender the mind to movement."

"Are you good at it?" I ask doubtfully. I still can't picture him with his toes pointed, swirling around.

"It doesn't matter if I'm good. That's not why I do it."

I nod, chastised. I *am* being kind of mean, assuming that just because he doesn't have the body type of a dancer that it's weird he's doing it. I'm being stupid and narrow-minded, just like the kind of girls I don't like, the ones who rule out everything that doesn't exist within perfectly set boundaries of acceptable teenage behaviour. "I think it's cool," I tell him to make up for my judge-y thoughts.

Ashani and Michael are already at the café, books and bags spread out on one of the outside tables. They're talking about *King Lear*, our English text. I hate that play. Personally, I think he should have just left his stuff to charity and let his dumb, selfish daughters live as paupers. At least then the story would've been over quicker.

Ashani's got a notebook open in front of her and a pen at the ready. And she's puffing furiously on one of those e-cigarette things. I get a whiff of cinnamon in the vapour cloud that wafts over us. She sits with her back rod-straight and her shoulders upright, all attentive. I bet she sits like that in every class too.

Michael, on the other hand, is sitting back against his chair, one leg crossed over his knee, his hat pulled down over his eyes. I've sensed from the beginning that this guy is kind of chill, and now I'm sure I'm right. This is good. We're going to need it to offset Ashani, because I get the feeling she's going to be even worse today. Peter announced yesterday that the three best performances from this project are going to be used in the Parent Showcase. That's some show they put on every term in the auditorium, apparently, showing off what the students have been doing. It showcases everything from drama and dance to debating, writing (people read poetry), music, and even gymnastics. Ashani really wants us to win one of those spots. I, on the other hand, do not care. I'm terrified enough of performing whatever we're going to do in front of the rest of the class.

Michael gives me a wide smile as I settle into a hard plastic seat. "Ms Zel. How was your day?" Antony just gets a half nod as greeting. I can't tell if it's boy-version chitchat or actual tension.

I'm just about to reply with my dream of a day when statistics cease to exist when Ashani interrupts. "Okay, we should get started."

"Where's Stella?" I ask.

Ashani dismisses me with a hand wave. "She'll be here," she says like it's normal. Which, so far, I guess it is.

As soon as the surly waitress with a picture of a guinea pig (why?) on her T-shirt takes our coffee orders, Ashani taps her pen on the page. "Has anyone come up with an idea for a theme?"

"We have a theme, don't we?" I ask, playing dumb. I can't help it. "Home, right?"

She draws in a breath. "Well, of course we have that as our *guide*, but we need something more specific, something more developed than that."

"Right." I sit back. This could take a while.

"So?" She looks around at us all.

I shake my head. I've had a hard enough time coming up with the concept for my photography project. There's been no time to hatch an idea for something we don't have to come up with for another couple of weeks. Have I mentioned that Ashani's getting totally ahead of herself? Peter says he'll be asking to hear our ideas at the end of the month.

Michael shrugs. "Sorry, Physics has been breaking my balls. But I'll be on it as soon as I finish this prac report tonight."

Ashani gives us a look which may or may not be recriminating. But now that I know I'm not alone, I elect not to give a crap. "Great," she says in a way that's clearly not great.

"I've had some thoughts," Antony says, leaning in, straightening his collar, and looking pretty pleased with himself.

I frown. Is it just me, or is my cousin happy that he's the only one who's done his homework? He starts talking about some poems he read this week. Ashani nods eagerly, her black-rimmed eyes fixed on his.

I listen for a minute but then tune out. It's amazing how much I already suck at this collaborative theatre thing. I'm staring into space when I realise the figure walking rapidly towards us is Stella. As usual, she's got her thumbs hooked in her backpack straps, and she's walking with that stiff-backed, high-necked walk that makes more sense now that I know she dances. I half expect her to be clutching a late note. At least the fact that she's walking fast tells me she actually cares about being late.

"Sorry," she mutters as she drops into the only available chair next to me and pulls off her backpack.

Ashani ignores her while Antony gives her this half wave. He doesn't stop talking, though. Michael grins and tips his baseball cap jauntily at her like some old-time dude.

The waitress slouches over to take her order, but Stella shakes her head. The girl glares at her empty notepad. I guess the fact that we're drinking precisely two beverages between the five of us isn't exactly good for business.

"What did I miss?" Stella asks me.

It takes me a second to answer. It's mostly the shock. I think this might be the first time she's spoken directly to me. "Only the fact that no one but Antony has an idea for this project yet," I tell her.

Michael gives her an *eek* grin and holds up his hands. "I had a physics test."

"Otherwise you would have been all over this, right?" Stella grins and pours a glass of water.

"Correct. So, how's things, Stell?" And he asks like he really cares.

I wait for her response, thinking I might be about to actually learn something about this girl—besides her fondness for fashionable lateness. But she just shrugs. "Alright. The usual."

He nods, like he knows exactly what the usual is. I, on the other hand, am still in the dark.

Suddenly Ashani claps her hand, Peter-like. I sigh. And here I was thinking school was done for the day. "Okay, so Antony's been reading some poetry he's found about homesickness in the early Australian colonies. That's an angle."

Michael folds his arms over his chest. "Let me guess: the poet's some long-dead Brit who was consigned to Botany Bay? Who wrote all about how he missed his cups of tea and walks in the woods with Gran?" He pulls a face. "Kind of obvious, right?"

I have to admit, I'm a bit surprised. Michael's so chill. I wouldn't have picked him to knock down an idea so quick.

"Not if we do something unique with it," Antony argues.

"But where's the social purpose in a homesick poet?"

Anthony actually bristles. I raise an eyebrow. I've never seen my cousin ruffled by anything. He glances at Ashani, looking a little smug. "I'm not saying it's a fully fleshed-out idea or anything. But it's something," he says pointedly. "At least I found *something*."

But Michael clearly isn't cowed by this reminder of his own failings. "And I'm just saying I think we can do better." He turns to Ashani and nods at her like he's sure she'll agree, mirroring Antony's look a second ago.

And that's when I put two and the suddenly screamingly freaking obvious together. This is not about the idea. Is it possible, I ask myself, that these guys are embroiled in some sort of macho drama poser match over Ashani? Because *that* would be something.

I turn and appraise her with new, slightly stunned eyes. I guess she's attractive in that theatrical diva style, with her thick ring of eye make-up and piled-up hair. But she's *so* bossy. But hey, maybe that's what they like. Who am I to question it? I'm clearly into cranky girls. The heart wants what the heart wants, right?

Ashani waves a hand at them and takes an extravagant puff of her stinky cinnamon thing. "We'll figure it out. It's just the beginning of this brainstorm."

It is? This is going to be one *long* assignment. But at least I now have a potential love triangle to amuse me along the way.

Ashani passes her latte to Stella. "Stell, got any ideas?"

"Not a single clue." She takes a sip and passes it back.

Ashani turns on me, the tip of her fake cigarette resting on her bottom lip. "You?"

I stare at her for a long second. "Once more, my name is Zel," I say slowly, as if I'm talking to a mildly stupid person. I can't help it. I'm usually pretty easygoing, but something tells me not to let this girl go all alpha on me. She hasn't actually done anything that I can see to earn this sense of superiority. Why should I pander to it?

She immediately corrects herself. "Sorry, Zel. Any ideas?"

The fact that she's willing to take a note makes me like her a *little* better. "Not yet, but I like what Peter was saying the other day about Nabokov. How he wrote to reinvent the home he lost."

"Yeah, that was interesting," Michael nods. "But isn't he just another homesick white guy?"

"Right, I got it. No homesick white guys."

He shrugs and lounges in his chair. "We've been hearing about sad white guys forever. Let's give someone else a shot." He smiles at me. I smile back. It's not as if he's wrong.

Stella nods and runs a finger around her water glass. "What about something to do with refugees? That's all over the news right now, so it's important."

Ashani sits even straighter, which I didn't know was possible. "Yes! Then we'd definitely have our social purpose."

Antony, eager now that Ashani's endorsed something, chimes in. "Yeah, the whole idea of being forced to leave home to survive."

Ashani turns to Michael. "That's what happened to heaps of people in your community, right?"

"My community?" He raises an eyebrow. "My parents came over so my dad could teach engineering at a university. We're not *all* refugees, you know."

"I'm sorry," Ashani says quickly. She actually looks embarrassed. I can't feel too cocky about it this time, though, because I might have made the same mistake.

"It's cool," Michael says. "But don't make assumptions, okay?"

Ashani nods. Her cheeks are a little pink, though.

Antony to the rescue. "I still think it's a good idea, though." He turns and smiles at Ashani.

"I do too," Michael quickly adds. "It really is a good idea." He also smiles at Ashani.

I shake my head and wonder if anyone remembers it was actually Stella's. She doesn't seem to care, though. She's just watching them talk, her arms resting on the edge of the table.

"It could definitely work," Ashani muses. "Once we hone in on an angle."

I fight the urge to sigh. I thought refugees *were* the angle? "Well, we've got time," I assure them. "Let's take some days to think about it. Maybe do some reading and meet again." I say this mostly because I'm hungry and I want to go home and eat the leftover curry I know is sitting in the fridge. And maybe I want to get away from Antony and Michael's lovesick chest beating. It started out amusing, but now it's just dragging things out.

"Yeah, I gotta go too," Stella says, picking up her backpack.

"Okay, let's all come to the table with ideas next week," Ashani says, looking meaningfully at me.

I ignore her jibe. "See you."

The others head off for the bus stop. That leaves me and Stella. Still, I'm surprised when she falls into step with me. I'm used to her taking off the minute we're done.

"I usually ride to school," she tells me. "But my bike's got a flat tyre."

I nod, kind of shocked by all those words. All for me. "That's a good idea," I finally say. I never thought of riding to school. Possibly because I'm a klutz. I don't think I've been on a bike since I was ten.

We walk along in silence, me trying to keep up with the pace. I'm kind of a leisurely walker, but Stella walks like Ashani runs meetings, quick and fierce. And just as I'm trying to figure out if the silence is awkward or not, she suddenly pipes up. "So, which of them do you think will win?"

I frown. "Win what?"

"The heart of our fearless leader, of course."

I laugh. "So I'm not the only one seeing that?"

"God, no." She shakes her head and gives me the closest thing I've seen to a real smile. "This has been going on forever. The only thing I can't figure out is if she knows or not."

I nod, still grinning. I did wonder the same.

"But I don't want to ask her either, because then I'd have to hear about it all the time."

"Are you two close?"

"Yeah, I guess. We've known each other since primary school. Ashani's kind of full-on, but she's a good friend."

"Full-on is right. Do you care that she got the credit for your idea?"

"It doesn't matter. Besides, it wasn't her. It was her boy stooges."

"True."

"You definitely put her in her place back there."

"I did?" I ask hopefully.

"As much as Ash can be put in her place."

"Yeah, well, she's a little bossy for me."

Stella smiles. "That's her natural state. She's a good person, though. And she'll make sure this project's perfect. You'll see."

We fall back into quiet as we turn a corner, away from the noise and the smoke-spewing buses of Bakers Road. Again, I can't tell if it's an awkward silence or just silence.

She slips a hand into her pocket and pulls out her phone, letting out a small hiss as she stares at the screen. "Crap, I'm late. I've got to go. I'll see you." She takes off at a run.

Of course she's late. That's her natural state, I think, as her skinny legs take her surprisingly fast down the street. I relax back into my normal snail's pace and think about the assignment. I decide that when I get home, I'm going to heat some curry and Google the hell out of some stuff. Ashani might be a taskmaster, but I do have to admit, my contribution has been a little thin so far. I'll make up for it with some serious research.

~ ~ ~

At least that's what I'm planning to do until I open the letterbox and find the envelope with Prim's scrawl on it. I stand at the gate and just blink at it for a while, because that's all I'm suddenly rendered physically and mentally able to do. What will it be this time, I wonder? Maybe some actual words.

Fumbling for my keys, I finally find them and shoulder the front door open. In the kitchen, I pull myself onto the bench and slowly tear the envelope open. Inside, I feel something soft and tissue-y. Okay, not a photo. I slowly draw out a blue and white striped napkin. I recognise it immediately. It's from a weird little diner we ate in a few times near our meeting spot. We loved their potato hash and the mumsy, funny woman who manned the counter and always told us off for something every time we came in.

I turn the napkin over, unfolding it gently and turning it around in my hand, hoping for a message. Nothing.

Sighing, I drop it onto the counter and try to hold back tears. Why won't Prim just send me words instead of photos and objects, forcing me to guess at their meaning? Last week it was an old subway token. The week before it was a brochure for the Bronx Homing Pigeon Club. It's like she's trying to remind me of us, but she doesn't want to engage either. What am I supposed to do with that epically mixed message?

I kick my legs against the cupboard and give way to the tears. I mean, why not? I'm confused as hell, and I don't know what she's trying to tell me—or *not* tell me—with these weird gifts. I'm sick of constantly sliding back and forth along the scale between confused and heartbroken and never having a clue where she is at. Prim's never been God's gift to effective communication, but if there was ever a time for her to say something concrete and real, it's now. Instead of all this meaningful nothingness.

CHAPTER 10

Maybe it's because I'm an idiot. Or maybe it's because I love to torture myself. Whatever it is, I don't do my Drama research after getting that gift in the mail. Instead I choose this miserable night to look at the first contact sheet from the subway project. The one I tried to hide from Stedman. I smooth it out on the empty kitchen table and lean over it. The first good photograph I pick out in a row of fairly average (bad lighting) ones is of a solitary cleaner pushing a vacuum past the door of a mall.

And it comes like a flash, the way I remember that mall so vividly. I don't even need the photos to see it. It was in Flushing. Our first trip. Like I said, before that, my only association with that neighbourhood was from cable reruns of a nineties sitcom about an obnoxious nanny who came from there. She and her family were really loud and nasal. They joked about being Jewish and constantly dressed in garish outfits. I guess I was expecting a whole neighbourhood of people like that, which shows how clueless I was.

As we emerged from the subway in Flushing, we were instantly assaulted by the usual New York cacophony of traffic and shouting and sirens and crowded sidewalks. But added to that was a visual assault of signage, mostly in vivid neon colours, nearly all in Chinese.

"I forgot there was another Chinatown here," Prim said as she set off down the street, dodging street vendors and shopping carts as casually as if she'd been here before.

I stumbled behind her as I stared around me. Like Manhattan's Chinatown, the area smelled like a combination of five-spice and old market vegetables. There were people everywhere, calling out to each other, hurrying down streets, and surveying the many millions of things that seemed to be for sale on this strip.

I'd always thought of Manhattan as the centre of it all, but it was as if travelling twenty minutes on the subway had made the world *more* alive rather than less.

Excited by our unexpected (well, I was such an NYC virgin that anything other than Midtown would have been unexpected at that point) find, we strode down the street, staring at everything. As we wove though the crowds of shoppers and commuters headed for the subway, airplanes roared over our heads on their way to the airport. They were so loud and low, they felt like they were just metres above my head. I held my breath each time one passed.

"Look." Prim pointed at a grim-looking block of apartments. The sign at the front said, *Bland Housing Estate.*

I grinned. "Unfortunate name." By this point, a light drift of rain was falling, and the clouds hung nearly as low as the planes. It was the perfect backdrop for this brownstone building with its rusted bar windows. I pulled my camera and snapped my first picture of the project, hoping it looked as bleak in the photo as it did in reality.

"I know, right? I wonder who lives there."

Of course that set us off on one of our story-making frenzies, trying to imagine the sad lives of the occupants of the place. Then we roamed through this mystery neighbourhood, turning down streets whenever we felt like it, adding parts to our story. I remember how unafraid we were to get lost. I learned that from Prim. She taught me that you can walk in New York without thinking about where you are. And then when you do want to know where you are or how to get back, there'll nearly always be a street number or a bus or a subway stop to take you back to familiar ground.

We found the mall later, in the afternoon. Even with this black-and-white contact sheet, I can remember the garish palette of that place so well. How the pinks and yellows and oranges clashed with the barren mood. It was like a ghost mall, in total contrast with the busy streets outside.

We stood there, staring through the sliding glass doors. That's when I snapped the photo, as a cleaner in a yellow flowered apron pushed her hoover across the bright-orange carpet. Without even discussing it, we walked inside. Because that's where Prim and I always matched best: in our insatiable curiosity for strange places and strange people. It's like we were both dragged in by the same piece of invisible string.

You know those movies where there's been an apocalypse or a war or a disaster and the survivors come up from underground? And they're surveying their world, still the same but empty of human life? That's what this mall felt like.

The place smelled like burnt sugar and old carpet. Neon signs flashed in stores and on games machines, and the lights shifted constantly. But at the same time, the place was this one big hush. There was tinny mall music coming from somewhere, but the volume was muted, and it was more like you sensed it rather than heard it. The staff in the shops just stood there, bored, or snuck glances at their phones, barely registering our presence. The only other sound was the rhythmic thwacking of a machine near the doorway, shooting at intervals some kind of fried, doughy treat out of a stainless steel tube.

"It's a freaking ghost town," Prim whispered as if we were in church and it would be indecent to speak any louder. "It's amazing."

I nodded and lifted my camera again and again, trying to catch everything.

"Where is everyone?" Prim stared up at the moving escalator, empty of shoppers.

"Maybe it fills up later."

"Nah." She shakes her head. "It was crowded an hour ago. The shopgirls murdered everyone."

Used to this kind of conversation already, I just nodded and took more photos.

"And we're next," Prim said as we stepped onto the escalator to explore the rest of the place.

Looking back, I feel like that first trip was not just a test of the subway project, it was a test of our friendship potential. And we passed with flying colours. By the time we were eating noodles in a steaming little cafeteria-like restaurant with the steady drizzle having turned to outright rain, we were already halfway there. While we waited out the downpour, Prim grilled me about my entire life (because once she decided she wanted to know someone, it was like she was insatiably curious). I even learned a tiny bit more about her. Not much, but enough. I learned she lived with her mum in Brooklyn. The crappy part, she insisted, not the hipster bits. (Not that it mattered to me. I didn't know *any* part of Brooklyn.) I also found out she had a cat and that she had no friends at school because she hated everybody. That's when she told me about her parents splitting and her dad moving away.

She told me all of this so matter-of-factly, it was like she was telling me about the weather. And maybe it was because I'd already got the sense that she didn't share much. Each little piece of information felt like something bestowed. And by the time we jumped back on the train, we were already talking about what line we'd do next. It was a given. We were doing this now. The subway project was a thing.

I scan the contact sheet, moving to other pictures from that trip. There is a series from inside the mall. Okay, but nothing special. They couldn't quite capture the desolation we felt in that place. There are a few decent street shots. And there, at the end, is the one I have been waiting for.

Here's the thing with manual photography. When you take pictures on a camera that doesn't let you see the picture instantly, you can't know how it's going to turn out. You just have to take it and hope. I hated that at first, but Leo taught me to like it. He taught me that anticipation can be a delicious thing. He also taught me to use that uncertainty to make sure I tried to take as good a photo as I could. To control every factor I could control, like exposure and depth and focus. Because there are no second chances with manual photography. And sometimes, just sometimes, when you take a picture that has the potential to be *that* good, you practically pray it turns out as well as you want it to. And the one I am looking for right now did.

I snapped it as we were heading back to the subway in the rain, the hoods of our jackets pulled up over our heads as we ducked between awnings. Just before we clattered down the stairs to the subway, I turned and took one last look at Main Street with my camera. Streams of people strode up the street opposite, an anonymous mass of umbrellas and legs. Above them was a neon jungle of advertising signs and tangles of electrical lines. And then, right above that, was a plane flying low against a steel-grey sky, moving in the same direction of the crowds. Everything about the flurry and rush I'd experienced in Flushing was present in one moment. I snapped the shot quickly and crossed my fingers as I sprinted down the stairs after Prim.

And after months of waiting, I now know the picture is as good as I hoped it would be. Better even. The image is cut in half, practically. One half is taken up by all the signs and the frenzy of people moving up the street en masse. The other half is all raincloud gloom and this giant hulk of a plane dominating the sky above. It's the perfect composition. I'm so excited by this image so full of its potential I can't wait to get to the darkroom and develop the other films.

It was on the way home from Flushing that we chose our next destination. This time it was my turn. On the train, Prim spread the map across both our laps and gave me one of her rare, actually kind of sweet smiles. Infected, I smiled back, shut my eyes, and pointed. Our subway mission probably made no sense to anyone else, but bound by a book and our twinned, insatiable curiosity, it made perfect sense to us. I was all in.

CHAPTER 11

On Sunday afternoon, I'm doing what every normal Sydney teenager would be doing—hanging out with her friends, shopping for new clothes, and checking out the talent walking past at an outdoor café while working on my tan/caffeine addiction.

Okay, I think we all know I am lying. Besides, even if I wanted to go shopping (ugh) or check out guys (ha), it's not like I have any friends to do it with. All I have to call my social own is my parents and my merry band of Drama geeks, and they have definitely not promoted me to weekend status (except Anthony, but that's because he's family and he has to). Not gonna lie, it would be nice to have some friends to hang out with. Or to have actual plans.

So what I'm really doing is lying out on the back deck, catching some sun and flipping through the newspapers, looking for opinion pieces to analyse for my English homework. Mum's supposed to be relaxing, but she's on her laptop, and I refuse to believe it's anything but work mixed in with a little Words with Friends light relief. Dad's leaning back in a deck chair, snoring quietly, although he'll deny everything.

It's one of those days when summer is handing out some gentle, sunny days before autumn kicks in and it starts to get colder. Although I do suspect Sydney's winter is going to feel like a kind of a joke after New York. The deck wood is warm under me, and it's tempting to nap. But homework duty calls.

I force myself to read through the opinion columns and letters to the editor. Most of them are responses to the news stories this week about babies being born in detention centres. See, in Australia, our government passed this law a while ago that means people who flee wars and persecution and stuff in other countries and try to sail to Australia without visas will never be allowed to live here. Our prime minister says that refugees should apply to come here properly, because lots of people have drowned or have had to be rescued, and the smugglers take advantage of their desperation to get here.

So anyway, if they're caught, they get sent to detention centres on these islands outside of Australia. No one knows much about these places, because the government keeps it pretty secret. But what people do know sounds pretty bad. And now there are people who've been there so long that babies are being born there.

I don't know if it's just because I'm PMSing or because this stuff really is just really sad and awful, but I'm reading this letter from a woman who used to work as a nurse in a detention centre somewhere in Darwin, back before they sent people to the islands, and I'm squeezing back tears.

We're lucky, she writes. *Most of us, when we think of home, think of it with warmth, with a feeling of belonging. We think of a place that makes us happy, or at least represents some measure of safety and security. Imagine if the only place you knew as home was the complete opposite of this? Imagine being born into a place where deprivation, disease, and imprisonment was your only idea of home?*

I sit up without finishing the last few lines of the article. And in the wave of sadness, I also feel this ping of hope. Because I've found it. I've found our idea.

~ ~ ~

Ashani takes a long puff of her fake cigarette and nods. "It's perfect."

"It is," Michael agrees. "How'd you think of it, Zel?"

I look uneasily across the lawn. I'm pretty sure even fake smoking isn't allowed on school grounds. I stretch my legs out on the grass and tell them about reading the article. And I can't lie, it feels pretty good to finally contribute something. Now Ashani can stop writing me off as some useless appendage.

"How sad," my cousin says quietly when I finish telling them about the letter. "Imagine growing up there."

I nod and watch Stella trot across the lawn towards us. She tosses her backpack down and sinks gracefully onto the grass next to Michael.

"Did you just get here?" he asks her. It's morning break.

She nods. "I had a free first and second, though."

"So Zel has the perfect idea for our project," Ashani interrupts. She puts her fake cigarette away and begins to chew on her fingernails instead. I'm not sure which habit is worse.

I quickly fill Stella in on the newspaper story. "It made me think about the fact that what most of us think about when we think of home is something that some people never get to experience. I mean, what will these babies think of when they think of home?"

"That's good." She plucks at the grass, frowning. "I mean it's a good idea. The babies not so much."

"It was your idea at our last meeting that made me think of it," I say, hoping the others are paying attention.

Stella gives me a tiny smile. I smile back as the bell rings for the end of break.

"Okay," Ashani says, piling up her books. "We've got our idea. Now we just need to figure out how to translate it into a performance. Can you guys meet on Tuesday after school?"

"Dance," Antony and Michael say in unison.

Ashani frowns. "Well, I can't do Wednesday. After your class? We can meet then. Get some food and work out a game plan."

"It's a date." Michael groans and stretches. "We finish at six thirty."

"Awesome idea, Zel," Antony says. "I'll see you at dinner tonight."

I nod. The Italians are having dinner tonight. We're going out for pizza. Because we like to live the stereotype, Dad says. Even if the pizza place we always go to is run by a German couple.

I pick up my bag and trail the love triangle back toward the red brick school building with Stella. It's starting to feel like I should tack on "as usual" after that description.

"Where's your dance class?" I ask her.

"Not far. You live on Grange, right?"

I nod, shielding my eyes from the sun until we get into the shade of the building.

"I can pick you up on the way."

"Don't you have dance too?"

"I'm in a different class than them. What's your house number?"

"Fifty-four. You sure?"

She shrugs. Indifferent as always. "Sure. Why not?" Then she leaves me at the door, striding down the hall to her class. I head for my Psych lab, grateful to have at least one semisocial plan for this week.

CHAPTER 12

By the time the doorbell rings on Tuesday, I'm cranky. Partly because Prim wasn't online when I got home and partly because I'm sleep deprived from staying up too late last night to stare uselessly at my Statistics for Psychology assignment. Maths and I still haven't found any common ground. Might as well face it, we were never meant to be. And then, just to make sure I'm really cranky by the time we have to go and meet the others, Stella is fifteen minutes late. Surprise.

I should probably tell you I'm one of those uptight people who hates being late. I know it's kind of weird for a teenager. I know we're supposed to be all slack and sleeping in and making our own time, but I can't help it. It makes me anxious. And *really* I hate it when other people make me late.

So, by the time the doorbell rings, I'm not exactly feeling the friendly.

"Sorry," Stella says as I open the door. She chews on her lip.

I don't say anything, because I can't think of anything not pissy to say. So I just lock the door behind me and follow her to the gate.

She grabs her bike from where she's left it leaning on the gate and steps astride it.

"I don't have a bike," I grumble, shoving my wallet in my pocket.

"I'll give you a ride."

She's so skinny I'm pretty sure a strong wind could blow her over. I'm not sure I want to entrust my future to that physique. I'm not a big girl by any means, but I'm no featherweight either.

She shrugs. Because apparently, that's the only way she knows how to communicate. "We can just walk. But we're late."

"I *know* we're late. Do you actually know how *not* to be late?" I give in and climb up onto the seat, holding onto her backpack for balance.

"I couldn't leave until someone else got home." She sounds kind of angry herself, but I choose to stay on my high horse (well, highly uncomfortable bike rack, to be exact) and say nothing.

The good news is she's stronger than she looks, and she has no trouble pedalling for the two of us. Even on the uphill stretch at the end, she just pedals harder. It's kind of nice, feeling the air rush by and watching the sun turn Stella's hair this radiant amber.

And by the time we get there, she's only puffing a little. It must be the dancing, because I'd be dying. But because I'm still a little ticked off, I don't act impressed. I just mutter a thanks without waiting for her to lock up her bike and head over to the boys, who are sitting outside a café across the road.

The boys look kind of flushed and sweaty and like I might not want to get downwind of them. I plant myself on the opposite side of the table. "How was class?"

"It was good," Michael says. "The teachers there are amazing. Aren't they, Stell?" He says this as Stella sits next to me, leaving a large space between us on the bench seat.

She just nods, fiddling with the sugar shaker.

"Where's Ashani?" I ask.

He shrugs. "Don't know."

"Got called into work." Antony holds up his phone. "She texted. Emergency fill-in."

Michael immediately gets out his phone. He flips open the case and looks relieved. "She messaged me too."

I smile. Ashani's definitely not giving either of them the upper hand. She has to know, I decide.

And because Ashani's not there to keep us in line, we don't get much done. Instead they tell me about their dance class, a blend of modern and movement, apparently.

"We should incorporate dance into this project," Michael says, stirring a third sugar into his coffee.

Antony nods. "That's a great idea. Give us an edge over the other groups."

That sounds exactly like something Ashani would say. I'm not really sure why we have to have an edge over the others, anyway. It's not like this is a competition, is it? Oh yeah, that's right. It is now, thanks to the Parent Showcase. But there's the other slight problem, of course. "I think you're forgetting I can't dance."

"You don't have to," Michael tells me "Dance doesn't have to be all of it. Anyway, I thought you'd love getting out of the performance part."

I sigh extravagantly. "If only."

"You don't have to perform, you know," Stella tells me.

"I don't?" I stare at them.

"Nope. As long as you do some important role, Peter won't care," Antony says.

"Really?" I want to grab them and hug them, I'm so relieved. "I'll do whatever I have to do if it means I don't have to go on actual stage."

"You'll have to for one of the projects through the year, though," Michael warns. "It's a rule."

I wave a hand at him. I'll worry about that later. "What can I do?"

"Well, Ashani will direct, I guess. She usually does."

Of course she does.

"What can you do?" Michael asks.

What can I do? "I take photos," I finally say.

"They're great too," Antony tells them.

"I've got an idea." Michael sits up. "We could have images projected behind us."

Stella sits up. "Yes."

I nod. "I could find images easily. Pictures of places that people have had to call home." I start mentally flicking through the news and photography sites online where I know I could find the kind of stuff we're looking for.

We agree to meet again at lunchtime tomorrow and tell Ashani our idea.

By the time we leave, we're pretty buzzed with our idea. When it's time to go, though, Stella doesn't say anything to me, just leaves me there with the boys and takes off on her bike. I guess she must still be mad.

~ ~ ~

When I get to the lawn at lunch, Stella's already there. She's crunching an apple and reading a textbook, busy being very incredibly not late.

I sit down next to her and pull out my lunch.

"You can say it if you want."

I can't help smiling. "Well, it *is* kind of a miracle."

"I know." She looks at her book for a long time. Then, just as I'm shoving some sandwich in my mouth, she mutters, "Sorry about yesterday."

I just nod, partly because my mouth is now full and partly because I don't know if she's apologising about being late or about riding off. Either way, I accept it, because what's the point in staying mad? That's not my style. Besides, we got there in the end, and we came up with an awesome idea.

She looks down at her book again, and I think she's done talking, so I start dreaming again.

"See," she suddenly says, "I've got a little brother. He's seven and he's autistic. Like, serious autistic. And he has to have someone with him all the time. We all take turns to look after him, but sometimes it gets hectic and not everyone gets home when they say they will be. Because the others are at uni and work and stuff, I look after him more than anyone. And sometimes he'll only respond to one of us. That's also why I'm late a lot. Yesterday, my older brother actually got home from uni on time for once to take over, but then Ollie—that's my little brother—wouldn't let anyone else get him out of the bath but me."

I nod, not sure what to say. I feel terrible, of course.

"And when he's totally fixed on something, he gets really, really upset if you try and change his mind. Sometimes it's just easier to go with it and do what he needs you to do, you know? I was late because I was getting him out of the bath and getting him ready for tea."

"I'm sorry."

She shrugs. "You didn't know."

"I know, but still."

"I just don't want you to think I'm this total slacker. I'm not."

"Okay, I promise I won't think that you're a slacker. Anymore." I grin and pick up my sandwich.

She smiles back. Her eyes are an incredibly light shade of blue in the sunlight. She returns to her book.

I sit there chewing and feeling bad and watching the others walk slowly toward us, discussing something furiously. I guess they all know about Stella's brother, which must be why they never say anything when Stella rocks up halfway through things.

Ashani's only a little miffed when we tell her we came up with the next part of the idea without her. But I can tell she can't get properly mad because she knows it's good.

"Stella's going to choreograph it," Michael says.

"I'm going to try, anyway," Stella replies. "Marina, my teacher, said she'd give us some advice."

"And Zel's going to find images to project behind it," Michael adds.

Ashani nods. "What about sound?"

"I could start looking around for some music?" Michael suggests.

"What about words? Could you move to words?" Ashani leans forward, frowning.

"I guess. Why?"

"What if we recorded stories? Or interviews? Or some kind of sound bites? And combined it with the movement and the images."

"That'd be a lot to take in at once," I say.

Ashani pulls a face. "So? It should be. Remember the social purpose. I mean, this is the kind of idea you want to punch home, right?"

I nod. She's totally right.

She starts talking about how all the elements could combine, how long it should take, and where everything should be positioned. And then she immediately starts anticipating any problems and challenges, all these little details I wouldn't have thought about until they happened. I'm starting to see why she gets automatic director rights. She's got this eye for both the big and small picture at the same time.

I'm definitely little-picture girl. My Lit teacher once told me I had this incredible talent for picking out the littlest thing in a book and recognising its symbolic significance but completely missing really obvious points. To this day, I don't know whether it was a good thing or a bad thing. Maybe that's why I love photography, which is, when you think about it, the ability to single out a detail and focus on it.

The end of lunchtime bell rings, and Ashani sits back and drums excitedly on her pile of books. "Okay, so, we're amazing, and we're going to murder this assignment."

We laugh. We laugh because she's being ridiculous. But I know we're also laughing because it feels like something we just might pull off. And it's something that might just be good too.

And this time, we walk back into school together, planning the next week around our project and cracking jokes. For the first time, it feels like these people might actually become my friends.

CHAPTER 13

I wonder if Prim would like the kids in the Drama group. Who knows? She'd probably have refused to meet them, anyway. Prim never wanted to meet my friends. And she definitely didn't do groups. In fact, besides me, she didn't really do people. Most of them, she said, were a waste of space. Sometimes her total intolerance was useful, like when creeps approached us on the street. She could get rid of them in seconds. But sometimes she was too quick to cut people off. She barely gave them a chance.

I remember once we were heading into the subway, on the way back from our trips, and I dropped my MetroCard on the steps. This guy tapped me on the shoulder and gave it back to me. I made some crack about needing to replace it once a month anyway. Seriously, I was more regular about losing MetroCards than I am with my menstrual cycle. Anyway, there was some hold-up with the trains, and this guy and his friend started chatting with us. Well, to me. Prim opened up an abandoned newspaper and completely ignored them. I mean, obviously, I wasn't interested in them, but they were nice, and they weren't being weird or gross or anything. They were these geeky, sweet students who were visiting for the week. They kept looking at Prim too (who wouldn't?) as they chatted, trying to include her, but she just would not engage. Just before the train was arriving, one of them started to offer up this invite to a party they were going to in Brooklyn on the weekend. He was doing the whole "if you're not doing anything" routine when Prim held up her hand.

"Don't even bother," she said without looking up. As the train pulled up, she grabbed my arm and stood. "We're going to that car." She pointed at one to the left. Then she pointed right. "And you're going to that one."

As I followed her to the train, I lifted my hands up and mouthed an apology to them. They just shook their heads and obediently got into the car she'd pointed to.

I elbowed her as we settled in next to the door. "That was a bit harsh, wasn't it? They were nice."

She shrugged. "Were you going to go to that party?"

"Well, no." As if my parents would have let me go to a party in Brooklyn.

"Then why bother?"

"They weren't doing anything. They were nice."

"They were boring."

And that was the end of that. Sometimes I wanted to tell her she was going to end up with no friends if she talked to people like that. The reason I didn't bother was because I didn't think she'd actually care.

I know I make Prim sound like she's kind of a bitch. And she could be. To others, anyway. But she's as loyal as all get-out when she's your friend. And she can be kind of sweet too, in her own backward way. She even did compliments. Not in a sucky way like the girls at school. ("You look so cute in that skirt." "That shade of lipstick is *slaying*, honey." Okay, none of that was said to me, exactly, but I don't really do skirts or lipstick. I heard that stuff all day, though.)

Prim's compliments were different. They were almost shockingly matter-of-fact, and they came at you out of nowhere. I remember when I first told her about Beth and Keeley, my only friends at school. I was telling her how nice they were, but how I didn't really feel like I connected with them. Not like I did with my old friends in Australia, anyway.

"Yeah, that's because they're the all-American, happy-clappy Christian types." She shoved a fry into her mouth. "They sound like something out of a TV show. Dull but sweet. You're way too intelligent to hang around with them," she said in her usual cutthroat way.

That's the way Prim did compliments. Just dropped them in right between her daily truth bombs and character assassinations. That time, I just laughed, but I was definitely flattered. Of course I had no intention of dumping Beth and Keeley. For one, I'm not merciless like Prim. But also they were sweet, even if they did bore me a little. And they were nice enough to befriend me while everyone else smiled politely and disregarded me. I liked the fact that Prim thought I was intelligent, though.

In true Prim form, she could give compliments, but she couldn't take them. If I ever alluded to her looks or said anything nice to her, she'd just cock an eyebrow and change the subject, like it was irrelevant. Maybe it was.

But was Prim a typical mean girl? I thought about this a lot. I know she said awful things about people sometimes, but she wasn't two-faced. She never did the whole nice to people's faces and then bitch behind their backs thing a lot of girls I know do. Prim was actually *no*-faced. If she didn't like something or someone, she just didn't engage, like the guys in the subway. She wasn't mean because I think being mean is something you do *to* people.

And it was Prim who gave me confidence in New York. She made me feel… *possible*. A mean girl wouldn't do that. One day, I remember I was complaining hard about how one of my school coordinators had marched up to me at school and just kind of announced—not *asked*, mind you—that I'd be giving a talk at a sophomore assembly about my life in Australia.

As you can probably guess from my total love of Drama class, talking in assembly is ranked up there with my own personal idea of a nightmare. But I was stuck with it. Because at this school, we had these things called "contribution points" that we had to earn throughout the year. We earned them by "giving back" to the school. Some kids earned them by participating in sports or debating or other extracurricular stuff. I had yet to find a way. The way this teacher was talking, I could basically knock out a quarter's worth with one talk. And I was already coming dangerously close to earning exactly none this quarter.

This was definitely not a good thing, because kids who didn't accumulate enough points had to come in on the term break and do jobs to "beautify" the school (read: scrubbing out lockers and washing windows). Apparently it was all part of our school making us better citizens. My theory is that it was all about cutting costs on janitorial staff.

So I was telling Prim about my sudden knifepoint speech task. We were on the train, steadily rattling our way uptown to a place called Woodlawn, where we would find a neighbourhood full of Irish pubs, bordered by a huge cemetery. There was something poetic or prophetic in that, but we couldn't decide which. We would wander through the cemetery for hours, inspecting each and every grave, looking for the youngest deaths and the most interesting, tragic, or strange inscriptions.

I kicked the heel of my boot on the train floor and pouted, completely caught up in my potential humiliation. "Didn't they even consider that public speech might not be my thing? Or that I might not even *want* to do it?"

"Of course they didn't. You're one of those people who seem like you can do anything."

My jaw literally dropped. "Me?" I asked, looking around me like an idiot, like I thought she was talking to some other person.

She shrugged and scrawled a lopsided daisy on the edge of her bag, then began to colour it in. I couldn't think of anything for her to draw that was more antithetical to her personality. "Yeah, because you're one of those people who just scream *capable*. You've got this totally not annoying confidence thing. So of course it'd never occur to those idiot teachers to think you might be nervous about something. Besides, even if you are, you'll do it anyway." She lifted her head from her drawing and stared at me. It was as if her fierce blue eyes were daring me to disagree. "And you'll be good at it too."

And that's when I realised Prim *saw* me. And she saw a me that I liked. A me who could do anything. That's how I used to feel back in Canberra before we moved, when I had my friends and my neighbourhood and a world I knew inside and out.

And I swear, because Prim said it was this way, it became that way. I believed her. She, with her pushy but impeccable logic, had that ability to convince me of things I didn't know.

"Okay, I'm just going to do it and get it over with," I said, doing a weak job of playing casual after that knock-me-sideways character reference.

"Of course you are." And that was clearly the end of that, because she turned to the window and rested her forehead on it, staring down the view outside. Prim could stare down a wall, I swear.

Anyway, that's the way Prim delivered stuff like that. Just dropped it in and walked away, bored and ready for the next thing. But I wasn't. I was still too stunned by her offering of this version of me. I think that's probably when I started to feel something for Prim too. Maybe it's kind of gross and into yourself to say that they first time you started to like someone is when they said nice things about you. But it wasn't the compliments that got me. It was the way this beautiful girl with her diabolical imagination and her messy charm noticed things about me.

It was Prim who gave me the idea of what to talk about at the assembly too. "Why don't you answer all those weird questions people are always asking you about Australia?" she suggested later as we wandered between graves. "You're always saying how the kids only ever talk to you about that stuff. Why don't you knock down all the questions in one go?"

I stopped in my tracks. It was the perfect idea. Because it's true, they did ask a lot of questions, and some of them were crazy misinformed. And they asked all the *same* questions about our animals, about beaches, or those clichéd questions like "Is it true every thing in Australia can kill you?" (The answer is yes, kind of.)

So that night, I went home and Googled things like "myths about Australia" and "questions people ask about Australia". I compiled a list and wrote down my answers. And when it came time to do the talk, I just put on my best give-no-shits Prim attitude and delivered. And everyone laughed and asked more questions, so it must have been okay.

So maybe Prim could be a bitch. But never to me. It was Prim that gave me the confidence to do that. And I started to love how being her friend made me feel. I know it's going to sound dumb, but her blunt faith in me, in my ability to do anything I wanted to do, made me feel like a superhero sometimes.

CHAPTER 14

Speaking of friends, Jason is definitely one of my favourite people at my new school. We don't really see each other out of art class except to wave and say hi, but at our corner table in the art room, we're like old mates. We talk about everything, from our lives, to art, to giving each other advice about our projects. We've extensively workshopped what it is exactly that makes Ms Stedman so intimidating. I already know all about his relationship with his girlfriend, Ruby, and he's the first person in school I've told that I'm gay.

Before you start thinking I'm all closeted and shy, it's not that. I don't care if people know. But I don't really run around announcing it out of the blue, because that's making it a thing, and it shouldn't be a thing. And at the same time, it's not the kind of thing that really comes up in small talk I make with other kids. I haven't even told the Drama group. Only because all we ever seem to do is talk shop. Antony might have told them, I suppose. I don't know. In some ways, I hope he has. I hate that awkward moment after you casually mention you're gay, and you clock the reaction, however miniscule. Because that's the thing. There's always a reaction, however small or positive. Why does there have to be one at all?

Jason's the kind of guy who can chat about anything. He can do deep, or he can do deeply shallow. He's seriously cool. His project is turning out to be beautiful too. He spent all his savings from summer work on a waterproof camera, and he's been taking his board out every morning and getting footage right out in the surf. It's incredible stuff.

And he'll do anything to get it, apparently. Because today, he comes in late with a gash on his lip. Stitches and everything.

"What happened?" I stare at the wound. "Ruby punch you for being a smart ass?"

He gives me a grin and then flinches, pressing a finger to the cut. "Very funny."

"Seriously, what happened?"

By now Stedman's joined us, probably to find out why he's late.

He pulls his laptop out of his bag. "I went out this morning to get some film. My board got into a fight with a rock. And I stupidly got in the way."

I have to laugh even while I'm cringing. "Ouch."

Stedman shakes her head. "Jason, your work is terrific, but I'd prefer you don't die for your art just yet. Be careful."

I practically stop breathing as I wait for her to turn to me and ask me where I'm at. But she doesn't. Instead, she's gone to check on the Instagram brigade.

My mouth drops. And this time, I'm not even relieved she's gone without questioning me. I'm convinced she's totally given up. Which of course makes me feel like a total failure. Twice more I neglected to cough up a satisfactory idea for my subway photos, and twice more she's told me to try again. Now she doesn't even ask. The last time we spoke about it she said, "Just keep developing the photos. Maybe it's one of those cases where the pictures are going to tell you what you need to know."

I just nodded, confused, and went back into hiding in the darkroom. And while her advice was *très* vague, I hope like hell she's right, because I've still got nothing.

But the good news is that she likes the actual photos. Most of them anyway. And she tends to like the same ones I like. She was super impressed with the Flushing airplane photo, which I'm afraid to report gave me that gross "teacher likes something I did" grin for the next ten minutes. It's definitely the best by far. There's a couple from Astoria I love too, these part-blurred images of people coming in and out of the doors of a pair of old Italian grocers. They're blurry because I didn't have my settings ready for the people rushing in and out, but it actually works in their favour. The blur gives a sense of the frenzy of it all.

My favourite picture from the bunch I developed during lunch yesterday is completely different. It's a shot of a crowd of old people, dressed in their best, streaming out of the doors of an old wooden church, the morning sun trickling through a wide green tree towering above them. There are people chatting on the sidewalk. Others are walking away from the camera, moving on to the next part of their day.

I'm looking at it again when Jason leans over.

"That's in New York?"

"I know, right? It doesn't look like it, but it is."

"That's not how I picture New York at all. It looks like you're in some small town in the middle of nowhere."

"It is, kind of. It's called City Island." I remember we felt exactly the same way when we discovered that sleepy little place. It was like we'd discovered an alien land.

~ ~ ~

It was the City Island trip where I discovered my crush on Prim too. It was just one tiny little thing that did it.

But let me start at the start. This time we'd picked the Bronx. A stop called Pelham Bay Park. Pelham was kind of underwhelming at first. The stop was one of those raised stops that you start getting further out into the boroughs. And when we walked downstairs and out of the boxy station building, we were kind of *meh*. It wasn't like Flushing, where we discovered a whole new world doing its thing, completely removed from the city we knew. It wasn't like Astoria either, where we felt like we'd discovered a little village unto its own.

Pelham Bay Park felt like one of those places that linger at the fringes of cities. They are a kind of bleed between areas. We were on one of those shopping strips under the rail bridge, and in the distance, I could see apartment towers and some trees. The immediate palette was steel, crumbled brick, and, of course, graffiti, but you could see a hint of a thinning-out into suburbia.

I'd seen on a map that there was a huge park right near this subway stop, but from where we stood, we couldn't see it. Couldn't even imagine it. All I could see was the same scene we saw everywhere on the fringes of New York. We stood outside the station, where the buses came and went, taking New Yorkers even further into the Bronx, not really sure what to do or where to go. There were signs pointing to places like Long Island and one to a place called Throg's Neck.

Then I noticed another one. "What the hell is Co-op City?" I wondered out loud, staring at a sign pointing to an exit. "It sounds so...orderly."

"Sounds kind of creepy and Stepford to me." Prim is obsessed with this old movie, *The Stepford Wives*. She gave it to me to watch. It's about this small town where all the housewives are turned into robots by their husbands so they'll be all docile and do as they say. It's totally creepy.

"Yeah, maybe it's just this land of apartment buildings built for robot people who come into the city and work every day, hypnotised to just do their eight-hour day and then come home and make no trouble."

Prim jumped straight on it, of course. "Yeah, it's a new master plan to keep the mean streets safe. These robot citizens will slowly infiltrate the whole city, starting in Pelham Bay Park, where clearly," she waved a hand at the dull view in front of us, "no one is going to expect a thing." She shook her head. "I bet no one even thinks about this place."

"Not even the people who live in it," I joked.

But something else had already distracted Prim. "Where's City Island?" she asked.

"How the hell would I know?" I was still too busy thinking about Co-op City.

"Look." She pointed at a bus idling at one of the stops outside the station. The City Island bus, according to its sign.

"Come on." She pulled the little black knapsack she carried everywhere higher onto her shoulder. "Let's go there. We *have* to go. It's a freaking island."

"But—" was all the logic questioning I could produce before she'd made a dash for the bus, jumping lightly up the steps, MetroCard in hand.

Ever the practical one, I wanted to suggest finding out how far away this mysterious island was before we got on. But it was too late. Prim was on the bus. So I shrugged and followed her, giving the bus driver a polite wave on my way past. We were going to City Island.

We were only driving for about three seconds before we hit a land of green. So *this* was the park part. We drove through this new world, crossing a series of bridges over water, and then before we knew it, the driver announced the last stop.

City Island kind of blew our minds a little. Even Prim was freaked. If Astoria felt like a village, City Island felt like a village fifty years ago. There was even a sign welcoming us to the Island. What? New York didn't welcome people. It tolerated them. Barely.

We learned later it was much busier in summer, but at that moment, on the cusp of the season, it was small-town dozy and sweet. The only thing that gave away its connection to New York was the view of skyscrapers across the stretch of water that led back to the city.

"Where the hell are we?" Prim asked in this hushed voice, her arms out at her sides as she turned in a slow circle, gazing around her.

"I have no idea." But I liked it. We wandered further along the avenue, gawping. I almost felt like we should tiptoe, as if we'd walked onto a movie set and we weren't sure if we were supposed to be here.

It was only moments after we arrived that I took the photo of the oldies in their Sunday best coming out of church. I couldn't help myself. One of them actually said good morning to us as he strolled past, I kid you not. That's when I remembered that in some places in the world, people go to church on Sundays and talk to each other, unlike my family. We go out to breakfast and sip lattes, studiously ignoring the rest of the New York crowds trying to do the same thing.

We explored the entire main street, from the churches and curiosity shops at one end, to the seafood restaurants where the fishing boats came in. Most of the shops and eateries were closed for the winter. We felt like we'd unearthed some kind of time capsule, a land that New York had forgotten.

When we were done exploring, we bought burgers and ducked down a side street, headed for the water that we kept catching glimpses of. The houses were wooden and rustic, with perfect lawns and gardens. *Actual* lawns, free of cigarette butts and rubbish and squirrel turd. I had to stop Prim from diving down in someone's front yard and laying in the fluffy grass. Some houses had flags flying from poles in the yard. I'd only ever seen that in movies.

"Jesus," Prim said, staring at them. "Makes me want to put my hand on my heart." Then she cackled.

We sat by the water, watching boats come and go, and listening to the small waves lap at the concrete wall. A breeze cut at the flimsy warmth of the sun and we zipped up our coats and tipped our faces up to absorb what warmth we could as we ate. Here, you could feel winter being left behind.

We didn't talk much. Prim and I could do that right from the start. It was cool, having this person to share these adventures with, but someone who I could also just chill with. Whenever I was with Keeley and Beth, I always felt like I had to be *on*. There always had to be something to talk about, something to do.

But Prim and I spent a lot of time sitting side by side, thinking hard, only comparing notes every now and then, like when one of us had dreamed up something funny or weird and we just had to share it. Or when one of us had a life question that became too pressing.

Sometimes we talked about everyday stuff, too. Like this time. Prim finished her drink, crushed the can between her palms and turned to me. "I love your hair colour."

I just shrugged, because I never really thought that much about my hair. I also shrugged because I couldn't quite fathom Prim finding anything physical about me worth talking about. Not when she looked like she did. Prim was a work of art. Prim was one of those girls who made every other girl feel immediately aware of their inability to even strive to something close to those kinds of looks. Prim was unfair.

Prim pulled a strand of her own hair from under the collar of her jacket and inspected it. "I thought about dyeing mine black, but your mum says I shouldn't." Then she reached up and took a strand of mine, holding them up to compare the colours. My bobbed hair was so short her face moved close to mine.

And that's when it happened.

Our science teacher taught us about Newton's theory, the one that said that for every action there is an equal and opposite reaction. I'm not so sure about that. Because sometimes the reaction is totally unequal. Just that light touch of Prim's fingers on my hair, just her physical proximity, set off a reaction that was in no way equal to the casualness of the action. Have you ever had that…rushing feeling? When a person touches you? It's like a kind of thrill that shimmers through you? That's what happened when Prim moved closer to me. It was so intense, I almost jumped.

What was happening? Well, okay, I'm not completely stupid. I knew pretty quickly what was happening. I just didn't know if it was my psyche having another of its horrible ideas. For a minute, I tried to write my reaction off to the fact that Prim never really touched me (as you can probably imagine, she's not exactly the touchy-feely type) and that I was surprised. But even minutes after she'd made her colour comparison, dropped our strands of hair, and was lying back on the grass, starring up at a scatter of clouds in the sky, I was still feeling aftermath rumbles. And I couldn't believe my own lie for even a second.

While her mind had probably moved to other, uncharted Prim mental terrains, my mind stayed stubbornly—stupidly—on that touch. I kept my face pointed forward, where Prim wouldn't be able to see my pink cheeks and horrified stare. I knew what this was. I had a thing for Prim.

Here's the thing, with girls I'd liked in the past: I'd known I liked them as soon as I met them. Or with Jonna, the first (and, okay, only) girl I'd ever kissed, we were friends who let something more happen between us one time. But this Prim thing was a total shock. How do you go from just innocently becoming friends with someone to suddenly feeling like this? Without seeing it coming? How do your brain and heart—command centres you're *supposed* to be in charge of—get to betray you like that? I just didn't get it. But as I stared out at the water, I knew I was stuck with it. Because right now, the only thing I wanted to do was lie back on the grass with Prim and weave my fingers through hers.

But I didn't, of course. Because I also knew I was now faced with a mammoth question. I had no idea if having a crush on Prim was something I even had any business having. I had no idea who or what she liked. She never talked about any of that stuff. And I wasn't sure I was brave enough to find out either. And I had no idea if she even had the potential to feel something for a girl. In fact, I knew nothing about Prim's capacity for love. Nothing at all.

When I finally mustered the courage to turn and look at her, Prim's arm was flung across her face, shielding her eyes from the sun. Her mouth was totally relaxed. And for all I knew, she could have been asleep. I felt a small stab of bitterness. How could she be so relaxed when my brain and heart were imploding? That, my friends, is the definition of unfair.

I had no idea how to find out Prim's potential either. I tend to make it a rule not to ask new female friends about their love life. I don't ask so they don't ask me about mine. So that the gay thing doesn't come up. Most of the time, I prefer to figure out if they are going to be cool or weird about it before I offer up that information. Call it self-preservation. Back in Canberra, some of the girls in my group definitely got weird. Just a few. They weren't exactly mean about it, but they definitely changed the way they talked to me. So now, with new friends, I wait before I tell them.

That day on City Island, I broke that rule, though. I had to know immediately if this was going to be futile, if I should resign myself to one of those destined-to-be-unrequited crushes. Because if it was, I could immediately shove it into that place where I stored hopeless crushes and get on with the business of being her friend.

On the bus back to the subway, I casually (I hoped) started in on my Prim romance recon mission. I tried to sound as offhand as I could as. "So do you, uh, have a boyfriend?"

She gave me a withering look, as if chastising me for stooping that low with her. "Why?"

"I was just…curious," I stuttered, playing with my camera strap so I wouldn't have to look at her.

"No." She leaned back in her seat and pressed a finger against the greasy bus window. "I don't date. Maybe if I ever met a non-stupid guy. But I'm not holding out any hope."

While my stomach got busy doing that doomy, sick-feeling thing, I nodded and grinned like I understood. There we had it, folks. Sexuality status: check. And of course I didn't feel any better for it. But there was that obnoxious, eternally hopeful part of me that thought maybe she hadn't found the right guy because she didn't know yet that she wasn't into them at all. I mean it was possible, right? That's what had happened to me.

If I wanted to know for sure, I was going to have to do or say something to find out. But that confidence Prim said I had clearly did *not* extend to girls. Most of my crushes so far had involved me developing a thing for a girl and then being totally crushed when I found out they liked a guy or, worse, started dating one. That kind of thing started before I even realised I was gay. Then once I did, I generally just made friends with a girl I liked. Just to be around her. It was safer. Easier.

That's what I did with Prim too. I friend-zoned her before she could friend-zone me. It was easier than being hurt. Or losing the only fun, amazing person I'd met since we'd moved here.

It wasn't until I was home that night, trying to get to sleep but too full of thoughts about my weird plot twist of a day to get there, that I realised something: Prim never asked me anything—not about boys, not about dating. And I have no idea if that was because she wasn't interested or because she'd already figured it out.

Chapter 15

Since we've moved to Sydney, a weekend where I don't hang out at home one hundred per cent of the time actually qualifies as exciting. But this weekend I went out twice. Did you read that? *Twice.* Watch out, people. I have emerged into Sydney society.

Okay, so maybe it wasn't quite that monumental. But it was nice to have something to do that wasn't sitting around the house doing homework, watching bad TV with Mum, or lying on my bed, trying to mentally will Prim to talk to me.

On Saturday morning I go to my new photography class. We don't do that much photography in art class at school, and I've been missing my classes with Leo, so I decided to sign up for another one. It's pretty different from my New York City program, though. That was only for teenagers. This class is at the adult education centre down the road, and everyone is about fifty years older than me. But it's the only one I could find close to my house.

And you know what? It turns out there's some untapped social potential in the over-sixty crowd. I have two new besties now—Miriam and Wayne. They moved here from Queensland. Their daughter hurt her back badly in a hiking accident, and her husband has some really important law job, so Miriam and Wayne are going to help with the kids. It's Wayne who tells me all this and a whole lot more while we wait for our teacher to start the class. Miriam, who's got this bright-orange hair, is too busy playing with the setting on her camera and muttering swear words. This is basically what she does for the entire class.

It was Wayne's idea that they do a photography class. He keeps lecturing me on how important it is to keep learning new things, even when you're an "ancient sack of bones" like him. I wouldn't have described him like that. He may have skinny chicken legs, but his belly could feed a small army. Wayne doesn't like digital cameras. He gets all tsk-tsky about them. "Lazy people use digital, Zel," he told me. "The kind of people who take shortcuts."

The first class is a little boring, all the getting-to-know-your-camera stuff that I already know. But still, I'm excited to take a photography class again. I've stopped taking photos lately, which makes me sad. I haven't felt like it much.

But after just one class, the itch is back. On Saturday afternoon, after class, I jump on a bus to Pott's Point and take some shots. But I feel kind of aimless, wandering around, snapping photos of "pretty things". I need a project or a theme.

Stedman's influence is getting to me.

On Saturday night, I go with Antony and the others to this talk at the town hall that Ashani found out about. It's an interview with this woman who's writing about Syrian refugees. It's kind of depressing that she's managed to write a whole book about it, and the war's still going. She's a tiny woman, dressed all in black but for her green headscarf, and she talks quickly in that way people do when they're really passionate about something. I don't understand everything she says about the politics, but the stories about the refugees—what they are living through during the war and in refugee camps afterward—I do understand. It was horrible and depressing.

When she's done talking, it's question time. Well, it's more like a whole lot of people getting up and giving their opinions on stuff and her giving hers back. It was kind of hard to follow from our seats at the back of the full hall. But one woman got up and said that she couldn't understand why, given the horrors so many people go through, Australia forces them into these island "prison camps", as she called them, and didn't take care of them properly. The writer said she felt like that too, but there were other issues at stake. I hoped she would say what they were, but the guy running the night ended the questions there.

As the lights go up, I hear Stella let out a little sigh next to me. I turn to look at her. I've been listening so hard that I've forgotten about the others. She's sitting there, her arms folded tight across her chest, her top teeth clamped down on her bottom lip. I guess she's as confused as me. As we walk away from the hall to the bus stop, everyone is kind of quiet, clearly too dazed by what we've heard. Even Ashani's silent, busily puffing on her fake cigarette. When we get to the bus stop,

Stella turns to the boys. "Can you two meet me at the studio tomorrow? We should start on this."

"While it's still raw?" Ashani asks.

"Something like that." Stella turns back to the boys. "So can you?"

Michael and Antony just nod. They're both frowning, serious still.

"Good." She takes a deep breath and climbs onto her bike. "I'll see you." The lights of her bicycle blend in with the neon cloud of headlights as she pedals off up the hill before finally disappearing into the glare.

When I get home, Mum and Dad are in the living room. Dad's watching some film, and Mum's half watching it over her laptop, the way she watches everything. I launch myself into an armchair.

Dad immediately hits pause. "Tell us about your night."

"Don't interrogate her." Mum pokes his arm. "Teenagers hate that."

"Something tells me we don't have one of those types of teenagers on our hands here. Zel's not like that."

I roll my eyes at them. "I'm right here, you know."

He laughs. "Nope, I'm wrong. There it is."

I smile, but soon retreat back to a frown. I still can't shake the unsettling feelings from that talk. "Do you think what we're doing to refugees is right?" I ask.

"What do you mean?" Mum peers over at her laptop at me.

"The detention centres. The people who come here by boat."

Dad keeps staring at the TV, but I can tell he's thinking about it.

"You know, I'm not sure, Zel. I don't like the sound of those places. The things we hear on the news. The kids there." Mum frowns. "But I also know it's a complex thing."

I turn to Dad. He nods, as if to say he knows I'm waiting for him to speak but hasn't quite got there yet. I wait. I want them to make some sense of it for me.

Finally he says, "We're not ignoring the crisis altogether. This country does take thousands of people with humanitarian visas every year. The government is just trying to stop the people who aren't going through the regular processes. To stop the smugglers who are encouraging people to risk their lives on boats to come here."

"But do they really have to lock them up in these awful places?"

He lets out a long breath and rubs his temples. "No, they don't. I think we could do more, and I think we could do better by these people."

I nod and scratch a pattern on the arm of the chair. I don't know how I would have felt if Dad had answered differently. I really don't.

"And I think maybe our politicians are too busy worrying about how to control the situation on their own terms that they've forgotten that these people are not the enemies," he says. "That these are *people*, people who have suffered enough hardship to want to spend all their life savings to get on a leaky boat that might be turned back or might not even make the journey. That's what makes me sad."

I jab my finger into the upholstery. "What do we do about it?"

"Find ways to let the government know you think it's wrong? Help these people in the ways you can help them?" He sighs, turning the remote over and over in his hand. "I just don't know, Zel. I really don't."

I'm not sure if this conversation has made me feel worse or better. I haul myself out of the armchair's comforting embrace. "I'm going to bed, you guys. Night."

"Night, kiddo." Dad calls after me. And I know he hates that he can't give me an answer. I guess there isn't one.

That night, my dreams are tangled and weird. The feelings from the talk are all messed up with other surreal dream stuff. I wake up around four in the morning and tiptoe into the darkened kitchen, gulping down a glass of water and hoping that by the time I go back to sleep, those dreams will have left me alone.

But when I pull the covers over my head and tumble down into sleep again, they're still there. Only this time, Prim is there too. She isn't doing anything much, and I don't even speak to her. But she is unbearably present. And I can remember exactly what it was like when I was around her.

I wake up, trying to hold the dream in my head. But it slips away, and all I am left with is this weird haunted feeling. All morning I try to concentrate on my homework, hunting out pictures for the Drama project. Here's the thing: When you're already miserable, combing the internet for images of homeless people and refugees is *not* a pleasant experience. But hey, that's my First-World problem, isn't it? That's what I kept reminding myself, anyway. Maybe I'm forced to look at it for a couple of hours, but I've never had to experience anything even close to that.

The other depressing thing is how easy it is to find horrible photos. Kids crouched on rubbish heaps where they spend all their days hunting for food. Families huddled in mud-floored tents, sheltering from weather and war. A corner of a park someone is forced to call home. It's hard too because even though this is the kind of thing we are trying to find, I don't just want to use these photos for the sake of shock value. It has to be meaningful. In this mood, I want our performance to be even better. I want to *do* something, to find some way to help. I don't want to be one of those people who just reblogs something or likes something and thinks that makes the slightest difference to anything. I guess this show we're creating is a start.

When I finish all my homework, I don't know what to do with myself. Mum and Dad have gone out with Uncle Rob and won't be back until later. The house feels empty. So I go out for a walk with my camera and snap a few photos. But again, I just feel aimless. And it doesn't help that it's one of those grey, slightly humid Sydney days and that the light is flimsy and dull. I give up and go home and spend the afternoon lying on my bed with my laptop watching YouTube clips of a new lesbian TV storyline I read about the other day. The characters are cute, and I'm intrigued, but I just can't focus.

My mind keeps returning to the dream and the feelings, and I can't shake the memory of having Prim so close. Even though I know it's pointless, I check to see if she's online. I even consider writing her an email. But I've tried that before, and I don't know if she actually reads them. I decide to write her a letter. Because I know she'll at least open it. She won't be able to resist. She used to make her brothers send her postcards, even though they lived in boring places, just because she loved getting mail.

I slowly scrawl a letter to her. I forgot how much I hate writing. My hand is sore before I've finished the first paragraph, and every time I change my mind about a word or a sentence, there's no deleting. I have to scribble it out and write again. Then there's the fact that I'm left-handed, so I get black marks all over the side of my hand where it rubs against the wet ink on the page. It's all so annoying. No wonder people invented computers. And it's so typical of Prim to love something that is basically torture for the person doing it.

I won't tell you what I wrote in the letter. Mostly because it's private, but also because it's all the stuff I've already told you. Basically I asked her to please, please talk to me, even if it is just to tell me to get lost. Because I need to know what she's thinking.

You know, in English we were reading this short story about the relationship between a husband and wife whose kid went missing five years before. They have no idea if their son is living or dead. The woman says she'd rather hear the news he is dead than to keep living with the uncertainty. I thought that was totally cold when I first read it, but now I kind of understand. It's this limbo with Prim that's worse than anything. I'd almost rather her tell me she never wants to see or talk to me again than live with the ambivalence of this silence. Almost.

Chapter 16

I come out late from Art class to see Stella sitting on the edge of the front lawn, eating her lunch. I hesitate, because I honestly have no idea what to do. I usually eat with the Drama group, but the others aren't there and the bell rang fifteen minutes ago. Stella's so hard to read that I don't know whether sitting with her or *not* sitting with her would bother her more.

Before I can make a decision, she spots me standing there, staring, and gives me a quizzical look. Then she raises a hand in a half wave. I give her a tight smile and pick my way between lunch groups towards her, relieved.

I throw my jacket down on the damp grass and sit on it. "Hey."

"Hey." She pushes a fork around the container in her hand. "Ashani forgot her lunch. She's snuck up to the café to get something. I don't know where the boys are."

"How did it go at the studio on the weekend?"

She contemplates a forkful of nuts and grains and green stuff and shrugs. "It was okay. It's going to take some time to capture the right feel." She drops the food back into the container and stirs it again. "I've never choreographed anything before, and I feel like it's super important to get this right, you know?"

I think of how sad and serious she looked the other night after the talk at the town hall. "That talk got to you too, huh?" I say.

"How could it not?" She stabs another forkful of salad. "It's all so messed up."

I nod, thinking of Mum and Dad the other night. How for one of the first times in my life, they couldn't give me a clear answer on something. Because it's impossible.

"I want to make sure the dance is as good as I can make it, and as meaningful, you know?"

"I feel the same way about the images."

She just nods and stares at her food, chewing slowly.

I point at her lunch. "Is the rabbit food a dance thing?"

She starts to give me a dirty look, but it softens into a smile when she sees I'm teasing. "Sound nutrition is very important. You should try it," she says in this haughty voice and raises a judge-y eyebrow at my lone piece of cold pizza.

I just shrug and pick an olive from the slice and pop it in my mouth. It was slim pickings in the fridge this morning.

"I'm half-Italian. *Flavour* is important to us."

"Yeah, yeah." She stretches her legs out on the grass and stares at her salad, frowning. "I *like* rabbit food."

"And you can keep liking your rabbit food, Stella." I catch a glimpse of Ashani on the other side of the lawn, sidling in through the school gate. She glances surreptitiously around her, clutching a greasy bag of chips. "As long as you're happy eating it on your own."

"I am. Thank you." We smile at each other and go back to eating our sad lunches as Ashani stomps towards us.

CHAPTER 17

It got so that Prim and I would meet every weekend or every second weekend and explore the end of another line. Getting us closer to our goal got us closer too. We started messaging each other about stuff beyond just planning our next trip. We spent hours trading our special brand of smart-assery back and forth. And we sent each other pictures, too, our own way of communicating. Soon, she was easily my best friend in New York. Of course there was that small problem of my outsized, so-far-unrequited crush, but I've become pretty good at keeping those things on a tight tether since I came out—teen queer survival mode. At least it is for me. Maybe some kids are lucky enough to grow up with other gay kids around, but the only ones I knew at my New York school were some boys who were way too cool to talk to me, even if I was one of their own.

Meanwhile, Prim and I hung out, and I kept my feelings on the down-low. Prim wasn't the kind of girl to take me into her confidence and tell me all her secret feelings like best friends are supposed to (surprise, surprise). That was never going to be Prim's style. The way she let me in was by showing me her life. By letting me see it for myself. That might not sound like such a big deal, but for Prim, I think it was.

I already had a sense her life wasn't as easy as mine. And when I finally was allowed at her house, then I knew it was true. Before the Bay Ridge trip, all I knew of Prim's family was that she has two older brothers from a different dad. They were both married and living in Long Island or Jersey or one of those places. Prim's dad left two years ago, and that was when Prim and her mum moved to Brooklyn.

I also knew her mum had become a little weird and paranoid since they moved to the city. *She hates the city*, Prim told me, and she missed her church friends back in Atlantic City. Her mum was convinced she or Prim were going to get killed. Prim had to message her mum every hour, practically, to check in.

I didn't even know where Prim lived in Brooklyn, exactly, until the day we drew her subway line. Prim picked it, stabbing into our next location with a stick I'd picked up off the damp ground in a little park in Norwood. When she opened her eyes to see where the stick had landed, on a line that ended in a place called Bay Ridge, she groaned. "Well, that's boring."

I gazed at the map as she pointed to another stop, two before the end. "See that stop? 77th Street?"

I nodded.

"That's my stop."

"Oh," I said. "Well, we still have to do it. Wherever we pick, we go." I'm not usually such a stickler for rules, but I was curious about where she lived.

"I *know* we still have to do it," she said, sounding tetchy. Then she tossed the stick at a tree and folded the map back up.

I think it was the rain that day. I don't know that she would ever have taken me to her apartment otherwise. We were walking around Bay Ridge, which turned out to be a bland neighbourhood on the edge of Brooklyn. Prim had read somewhere that this was one of the few neighbourhoods in New York where the rent had *not* tripled in the last ten years. I could sort of see why. It was a pretty depressing place.

When I left Manhattan to catch the R line that morning the sky had been clear, but by the time we had shared our sandwich and were ready to leave the crappy little diner in Bay Ridge, it was pouring. We bolted for the subway, but it was that kind of rain that hits you sideways and drenches you immediately. Like Sydney rain.

We stood panting and dripping on the subway platform. Prim wrung her hair out like it was laundry, dripping all over the platform. I checked on my camera, which I kept tucked into my little backpack inside a plastic bag. It was fine. Only then did I worry about me.

I shook myself like a dog to rid myself of as much of the rain as I could.

That made Prim laugh. "Okay, Spot. Calm down." She pushed her hair back behind her shoulder and considered us. "*Alright*, we'll go to my place to get dry."

It was funny the way she said "alright", like I'd been begging her and she was finally giving in.

"It's okay," I said hurriedly, even though I was curious. "I can ju—"

"Then you can meet Violet." Prim kind of wriggled on the spot. Her mood turned as sunny as Prim's mood can.

"That's the cat, right?" I asked cautiously.

"That," she said as the train roared into the stop in front of us, "is the queen of all cats."

Being taken to Prim's flat felt like some sort of privilege. The apartment was in a dead part of 4th Avenue, in a block above a shop. The stairs smelled like pee and mildew, but that's nothing new for the city. At least the lights in the stairwell worked.

I'd thought my apartment was small, but Prim's was *tiny*. She had the only bedroom, while her mum slept on a sofa bed in the poky living room. The kitchen was an alcove in the corner, and there was a bathroom I didn't see. The place smelled of cooking and damp. It looked even smaller because the blinds were drawn in the middle of the day. Prim came out of the bathroom and tossed me a towel.

"My mom's totally paranoid that people are looking in all the time." Prim rolled her eyes as she pulled the cord to open the blinds. The rain-washed grey light only cheered up the place marginally. But I could see now how immaculate it was. "She's also a total neat freak," Prim told me as she wrapped a towel around her neck.

I followed her into her room, where a sleeping cat was sprawled on its side on the bed. The blinds were closed in there too. "I tell her not to close mine, but she does it anyway. I don't want Violet to die of vitamin D deficiency."

I grinned. Did cats even need vitamin D? Not that I'd challenge Prim on it. I already knew that Prim's cat was a non-negotiable part of her. The cat loved her too. The minute Prim sat down beside her, it started pawing and purring, sounding just like a washing machine on spin cycle.

Violet is skinny and grey, with two different colour eyes, and she likes no one but Prim. At first, the cat just completely ignored me, but when I reached out to give her a tentative pat, I found myself dodging a swipe of her paw. After that, even staying as far away as I could get from her, every time I so much as adjusted my position on the end of the bed, she'd turn and hiss and swish her tail. That cat was a psycho.

Prim didn't say anything, just kept petting and cooing. Curious, I looked around the room. I couldn't help feeling, well, sad. Prim had *nothing*. The only things in the room were her bed, a dressing table with a couple of things on it, and a side table with some schoolbooks piled on it. I'd assumed she wasn't rich, what with a disappearing dad and a mum who worked as a cleaner, but I guess I never really thought about it properly.

Her jacket gathered pale hairs as she held the cat like a baby. I tried to tell myself it was just a minimalist thing. My friend Kate back in Canberra was like that. We'd always joked she was obsessive compulsive, because she *hated* clutter in her room. But what she did allow in her room was always nice and new and shiny. Everything in here was mismatched and old, even the textbooks.

I realised now why Prim always wore the same thing, those skinny black jeans, the boots, and a big army jacket. I guess I'd just thought it was the only thing she liked, but maybe it was all she had. I chewed on my lip, feeling kind of embarrassed and weird for paying attention to this stuff.

Where I grew up in Canberra, everyone was the same. In our neighbourhood, we all had pretty much the same stuff and the same lifestyle. Sure, there were a few kids whose parents coughed up for private schools or who got more pocket money than the rest of us, but I really wasn't used to thinking about this stuff. It was one of the first times in my life I was forced to check my privilege, to recognise it existed.

When Prim finally looked up from the cat adoration, it was like she'd been completely aware of what I was thinking. "This is why I'll do the modelling thing," she said. "I still think it's the dumbest job in the world, but the money will be good." She shrugged as if it were no big deal. "I really want a computer. I want to move out of here."

I just nodded, because I still didn't know what to say.

She lay Violet gently back on the bed, grabbed my towel, and took it to the bathroom. I followed her out into the living room, too nervous to stay with that devil cat. Again, I was taken with how small her place was. How claustrophobic.

I mean, our Midtown apartment was pretty tiny, but it wasn't just about space here. It was about being forced to live with the blinds down. It was about her mother. It was about living in such close proximity to someone, someone who worried about everything and projected those worries onto you. How could normal intrude on this weird, suffocating capsule?

Now I get why Prim loved our subway expeditions. They made her world bigger. Even in winter, when I started to complain about traipsing around in the cold, she was relentless. It was better than being stuck in that flat with a nervous mum and the blinds drawn.

For her birthday the following month, I bought her a little cactus in a stone pot. Partly because its prickly, pointy character was perfect for Prim, but the gift was also tactical.

"Tell your mum she has to leave your blinds open now," I told her as she held the little plant up and peered at it. "Otherwise it'll die."

She brushed a finger across the tiny spikes at the top of the cactus and grinned at me. "And that's why you're a genius," she said.

And like the besotted girl I was, I grinned back.

CHAPTER 18

The next Sunday, Ashani and I meet the others early at the dance studio. We have to be out before the regular classes begin.

The studio is in this boxy, brown brick building perched above a fish and chip shop. I find Ashani outside, trying to figure out how to get in.

She waves, her other hand pressed over a yawn. "Not a morning person," she mumbles.

I nod and look around for the entrance. Finally we find a metal staircase next to some garbage bins in a laneway at the side of the building. This is totally the kind of dump that I can imagine featuring in some famous dancer's biography. A "look where they started" rags-to-riches thing.

The inside is much nicer. Simple, with clean white walls, a couple of dance posters stuck around, and one of those bars that ballet dancers use wrapped around the room. That's it, really. The other three are here already, looking sweaty and tired. Well, Antony and Michael do. Stella looks fine.

When you see Stella in her dance clothes, she suddenly makes perfect sense: her skinniness, her perfect posture, that walk. Placed in the context of dance, she looks like she's found what she's supposed to be. I think she's happier there too, because when we arrive, she actually smiles. Not one of those "I'm supposed to smile now" teeth barings she usually favours, but an actual smile. I nearly fall over.

"Hey," she says as she swipes some loose strands of hair from her forehead. "Welcome to our glamourous place of work."

I smile back. More at her smile than her joke.

Michael and Antony are both sprawled on the ground.

I laugh. "I hope this isn't the starting pose."

"We haven't got too much done yet." Michael stretches his arms out above his head and grimaces. "We're just feeling some things out."

"It's tricky working without sound too. Without a beat." Stella rolls up the waistband of her leggings and kicks out her feet, like she's trying to loosen something.

"Maybe we can work a beat in with whatever we record to go over the top?" Ashani suggests.

Stella nods. "It would help, but we can make it work either way." She spins around and paces back to the corner. "We'll get there."

She takes a long drink from her water bottle and then drops into a stretch. I can't stop watching her. She's so chill and in her element today.

"So, do you want to see what we've got so far?" Antony asks.

"Well, I didn't get up at dawn on a Sunday to hang out in this brick palace for nothing." Ashani sinks into a chair and takes a dramatically long sip of her coffee. I roll my eyes. And it's nine, hardly the crack of dawn torture material she's making it out to be.

The others take their places in the middle of the room. And because Ashani's taken the only chair in the place, I sink down to sit against the wall next to her, my knees tucked to my chest.

They only dance for only a minute, but it's enough. They begin in a tight group, clustered back to back, sometimes flung apart suddenly and then pulled back together. Sometimes it's slow, and sometimes it's fast. Then they slowly begin to dance away from each other, stepping across the floor into separate corners, and turn back to face each other. There's not much to it yet, but you can already get an idea of what they are trying to convey. There's this sense of connection between them. You can see the ideas of protection and unity being played out without anything being said, you know? And I can't explain how, because I know nothing about dance. Just trust me, it's really cool.

The boys are better than I thought they'd be. Michael's pretty good, though he keeps forgetting the steps and having to hurry to catch up. Antony's not as good, but he has all the steps down already. And there's something about his strange kind of lumbering dance style that is oddly elegant. It's this careful energy he possesses. Whatever he does, Antony always holds this air of being so dignified, and it's weirdly beautiful.

And Stella? What can I say? It only takes fifty seconds of a half-formed dance to understand that Stella is a beast. Like, *amazing.* The boys look exactly like dance students, but she looks like a real dancer. In fact, the boys are lucky I looked at them at all.

I wish I knew the words to use to describe how easily Stella uses her body, but I just don't have them. Which is why when the routine dwindles to a halt, I'm slack-jawed. Here's the thing: I've never really *got* dance, but I also didn't know until now you don't really have to. You just watch it. And if it's good, it makes you feel it.

As soon as they finish, before even Ashani gets to say a word, Stella gets them to run through it again. The boys sigh but immediately obey. It's a strange new world in this studio, one where Stella is in charge. I'm glad, because all I want to do is watch it again.

As soon as it's over, Antony and Michael immediately flop down on the ground, catching their breath. Not Stella. She keeps moving, tacking on steps, only half-dancing them, like she's mentally composing the next part.

"What do you think so far?" Michael asks us. Well, he asks Ashani, really. Because I think we all know by now that those boys only care what Ashani thinks.

She looks seriously impressed. I think that's a first. "I like it. Very evocative."

I half listen to Antony's explanation of the dance, but I'm too busy watching Stella move. I do that thing that I always do when I see something that strikes me visually. I imagine how I'd photograph it. Suddenly, Stella seems to remember we're here, and stops. She wanders back to us.

Antony nudges my foot. "What did you reckon, Zel?"

They're actually asking me? I shrug. "Wow?" I try. "That's all I got, people."

Stella smiles. She's about to say something, but the door opens. A woman sticks her head in. "Time's up, folks."

Stella scurries over to pick up her bag from the corner. "We better go, guys. There's a class in here now."

We troop down the metal stairs into the bright morning sun.

While we're standing there, waiting for Stella to unlock her bike from the railings, kids and parents start to stream down the laneway. The little girls are all in leggings and tight buns. Mini-Stellas. Some of them call out to her and wave.

Stella waves back and then turns to us. She rolls her eyes and grins. "Baby ballet class time. Let's get out of here."

Footsteps clatter loudly on the metal steps above us as we stride down the laneway. I hope no one is trying to sleep in on this block, because it will not be happening.

At the end of the laneway, Ashani claps her hands and kind of gasps. "I've got it!"

"Got what?" Michael asks out of a yawn.

"What we should do for the sound part."

"What?" I ask, curious.

"You know how I said we should use voices? I'm going to go around vox-popping people ab—"

"Vox pop?" Stella asks before I have to.

"It's Latin for "voice of the people". Like, when you go up to random people and ask them questions." She kind of flaps her hand, impatient. "*Anyway*, I'm going to go and ask people what home means to them, and then when I have heaps of answers, I'll edit it all together into a soundscape."

"Hey, that's good," I say, running with it. "And then if the images I put together provide the contrast, it will be really jarring. I mean," I look around at them all, "we're assuming most people are going to say nice, warm, fuzzy things about their idea of home, right?"

Ashani nods. "Of course."

"So, while those people give their ideal version of what home is, the images act as the reality for refugees—the detention centres and camps and stuff." I think of all those photos I stored in a file. I could find a way to ease into those too. Start with nice homey photos and gradually introduce the harsher ones. I tell them about my idea for slowly transitioning the images from idyllic to ugly reality.

"That's awesome. The contrast between the sound and those images will be mind-blowing." Michael rubs his hands together.

Ashani nods, but she looks a little miffed. Maybe I stole her thunder a little, but I couldn't help it. I was excited.

"The 'vox pots', or whatever you call them, are a great idea," I tell her, giving credit where it's due. Only fair, right?

She livens up a bit. "I might go into the city right now and start collecting some." She tosses her empty coffee cup into an already-overflowing bin. "Anyone want to come?"

"I will." Michael pulls his backpack onto his shoulders and does a little jog on the spot as if to say he's ready.

"Me too," Antony quickly adds.

Gee, who didn't see that coming?

I look at Stella, eyebrow raised, but she's busy yanking on a hoodie over her tank.

"What about you guys?" Michael asks.

Stella shakes her head. "Can't. Sorry."

I kind of want to, but I don't want to be fourth wheel to this dysfunctional little triangle either, so I say, "No, I should get home and do some work on my part, actually."

I could catch the bus a couple of stops with them, but the sun's shining and there's only homework waiting for me back at the house. Perfect procrastination moment, methinks. I go straight into dream mode, thinking about the project, so it takes me a half a minute to realise Stella's wheeling her bike next to me.

Why does she always do that? And why am I always so surprised when she chooses to have anything to do with me? Oh yeah, that's right—because she's so freakishly silent most of the time. I guess the dancing has put her in a good mood. Or maybe, like me, she's excited by Ashani's idea for the sound. It's kind of pulled it all together. We now have the perfect way to make people think about all these ideas we've had, all this stuff we've been learning.

"This project might be amazing."

Stella gives me a curious look. "I didn't think you cared that much. You don't seem that into Drama."

"I'm not. Well, I'm not much of a performer."

"You don't say." She laughs. "I've seen you hiding in the back of every improv scene in class, you know."

I somehow manage to laugh and blush at the same time. Busted.

"Improv is *really* not my cup of tea. I stupidly let Antony talk me into taking Drama. I didn't know we'd be doing all that stuff."

"What did you think we'd be doing?"

"I don't know. Putting on plays, reading from scripts." I thrust my hands into my pockets and watch a giant brown dog walk a man across the road. "I like this project we're doing now, though."

"I kind of know how you feel. I hate talking on stage. It freaks me out."

"But you're completely happy to dance?"

"Yup." Then she shrugs as if to say *it is what it is*. Which it is, I guess.

"Well, you're an amazing dancer."

She doesn't smile, but she doesn't brush the compliment off either. "Thanks."

"Have you been doing it long?"

"I started ballet when I was six, but I only started contemporary dance two years ago. Then as soon as I started that, I quit ballet."

"Why did you quit ballet?" I'm genuinely curious but also thinking I should get whatever intel I can on this girl while she's actually, willingly, making conversation.

She gives me a weary smile. "I should warn you, I've failed to explain this adequately to anyone, *including* my old ballet teacher. She was kind of mad at me for quitting. But I don't know. Once I tried contemporary, I just started feeling like traditional ballet was like…this really clunky way of appearing fluid, you know?"

No, I don't know. But I nod anyway, just to keep her talking.

She steps off the kerb with her bike so a group of shoppers can pass. "And contemporary just felt really natural to me. I feel like my body can translate what it's trying to say better. I don't know how else to put it."

I definitely don't know the difference between ballet and contemporary, but I do know that in the studio, she looked so completely like someone who is doing what she is meant to be doing. So she must have chosen right. I tell her so.

This time, she does this cute chin-ducking thing and kind of smiles. And because she's being like that, I finally brave up enough to ask her the question that's been circling my brain since we were in the studio. "I was wondering: is there any chance you'd let me take photos of you dancing?"

She gives me a weird look. Blushing, I hurriedly explain about my photography class.

"Oh. Sure, then."

"Really?" I squint at her.

"Of course. Why'd you ask if you thought I'd say no?"

I'm stumped, for some reason, so I blush and stare at some boys in football uniforms, laughing and squawking about something, so I don't have to meet her eye.

She steps back up onto the footpath and nudges me with her elbow. "I'm just teasing. Of course you can. We'll just have to get some studio time. I'll let you know when, okay?"

"Okay. Th-thanks."

"But there's one thing I want in return." She gives me a playful smile.

I narrow my eyes at her. This almost bubbly, friendly version of Stella is confusing me. "What?"

"I want to see some of your photos. I didn't know you were a photographer."

I'm tempted to remind her that she probably doesn't know because she's not exactly been the most giving conversationalist until now. But I also don't want to wreck it or make her change her mind. So I tell her my Instagram handle.

Stella stops pushing her bike at the top of the hill on Bakers Road and pulls her helmet from the handlebar. "I better get a move on, or I'll be late."

"What are you doing today?"

"Taking my little brother to the pools. We go every weekend." She clips on her helmet. "He's addicted to water."

I nod, wondering what it'd be like to have a sibling I had to look after. Especially one that needs so much looking after. I've never thought about how lucky I am being an only child. I've really only thought about how much I was missing out on not having a brother or sister. But that's an only child way to think, isn't it? Only about yourself.

"Want a lift down the hill? You know I can do it," she teases.

I smile, tempted, but shake my head. "I better not. If we get caught…"

"True." She gives me a small wave. "See you next week."

"Bye," I say to her back as she begins to coast down the hill. I watch stray hairs fly out behind her as she picks up speed, and I keep walking. I'm happy she's turned out to actually be a cool person under all that silence. With the other three all caught up in each other, it's good to have an ally. Maybe even a sort-of friend.

As I trudge home, I think about the dance and Ashani's idea, and I pick up my pace. This time I actually want to get home and start work. I want to put together a montage that will be as amazing as I know the dance is going to be. I stride along the footpath, dodging dog walkers and shoppers, wishing now that I'd taken Stella up on her offer.

CHAPTER 19

We took a lot of trips that spring, me and Prim. I can't tell you about them all, so you'll have to imagine it like that montage in the middle of a film. You know, the one where time passes and you just see a bunch of scenes backed by some cheesy music: More trips, more subway lines, us getting a little closer. Me being more smitten. Lots of laughing and smiling and Prim being snarky. That kind of thing.

Pre–subway coffee became the ritual. Well, tea for me. We'd sit in the corner of a Starbucks (yes, I eventually caved), on a sofa if we could snag one, and compare notes on our week. And only when we were caught up and Prim was caffeinated would we go. Prim would tell me about her school, which, in her true melodramatic form, she made sound full of crazies and delinquents. According to her, the possibility of death or maiming was palpable every second. It's hard to know how bad it actually was, because I learned pretty quickly with Prim that sometimes it was hard to tell where reality left off and a total love affair with exaggeration began.

She asked me stuff too. For some weird reason, Prim liked to hear about Keeley and Beth. She had zero desire to meet them, but she still demanded weekly updates on the "the nuns". She liked hearing the mundane things about them, what they said and did and who they were dating. "They're so *normal*," she'd say, wide-eyed, as if discussing some exotic, on-the-verge-of-extinction creature.

She loved to tell me stories about her part-time job too, the one that kept her in Starbucks money, second hand books, and MetroCards. Two afternoons a week, she worked the counter at a laundry near her place, giving change and collecting laundry service that a small army of women came in overnight to wash and iron. I couldn't imagine Prim doing customer service. I mean, the girl had wicked snark game. Terrifying snark game, actually. But she loved this job.

"Better than working here, right?" she'd said, looking around the Starbucks we were sitting in that day. "Or serving fried food to people who are already halfway to their first heart attack."

She said she loved watching the people who used the self-service machines. Some were boringly normal, some were crazy, and some were flat out obsessive-compulsive. She told me about a woman who sprayed every single washer out with bleach every time she came in. Not just the ones she used, but all of them. Prim loved this stuff. It was fodder for that imagination of hers.

Of all the trips Prim and I took, the weirdest was to a place called Ozone Park.

It wasn't about the destination necessarily, which was a neighbourhood out on the edge of Queens. It was about all the things that happened that day. It was all such a strange combination of sad and funny and weird.

The first thing happened on the train going there. We were sitting in a mostly empty car, riding a rail that travelled over a flat urban sprawl. I was combing Instagram, and Prim, I thought, was staring out the window.

Suddenly she nudged me. "Hey?"

"What?"

She wrapped her hands around her narrow thigh. "Do you think my legs are bigger than hers?"

I followed her gaze up to an ad on the train wall. It was your typical jeans ad, a bunch of skinny, overly attractive people slouching around in denim. Prim would've fit right in. My mouth fell open. I never thought I'd hear a question like that come out of Prim's mouth.

She elbowed me. "Seriously, look."

I looked at her legs and the model's. Then I just shook my head at her and glared. "Prim, don't."

"Don't what?" She looked annoyed.

That didn't stop me, though. No way was I letting this slide. "Don't get caught up in that skinny crap." I grabbed her hand and yanked it away from her leg. "Who cares? You're skinny. Model skinny. Gross skinny." I saw a flash of shock in her eyes. "Don't focus on it, and don't start comparing yourself to other girls. It's dumb."

"Alright," she muttered, pulling her arm back. And you know what? She actually looked a little bit embarrassed. I was glad. I couldn't bear the thought of Prim thinking about that stuff.

Even after we dropped back into silence, I couldn't stop thinking about it. See, this was one of the things I'd always admired about Prim, that she didn't usually compare herself to other girls. Until now, I'd thought she had this amazing ability not to get caught up in the anxieties that so many other girls seemed to have, constantly scrutinising themselves or each other to see how they stacked up. Especially given how much Mum says that happens among models. I thought Prim was inured to that crap, but it turned out she wasn't. It made me feel uneasy and weird for the rest of the ride.

I forgot about it, though, for the first part of our afternoon in Ozone Park. It was cold and sunny, which helped. But autumn was edging into winter, even though we had been given this one day of grace from the grey.

Then we found the fence. It was this huge wooden thing, towering way above our heads. It dwarfed the house it surrounded, making it look like a miniature version of itself. It stuck out like a sore thumb, surrounded by other houses with low stone fences or with no fences at all.

Prim went instantly into story mode, making up her own reasons for the existence of the fence, when a voice spoke behind us, making even her jump.

"This been here for over fifty years." The voice came from a little old man. He was tiny, both in height and width.

"Why is it so crazy tall?" Prim asked, jumping up to try and touch the top. But not even her legs could get her there.

The old guy chuckled and said in his thick (maybe Greek?) accent, "To keep people out. Well, to keep one person out." He moved in closer and leaned against the palings.

"Who?" Prim asked, settling against the fence, arms crossed, ready for story time.

Once he started, it was easy to see why he wanted to tell his story. It turned out to be an epic tale. This old guy standing in front of us had lived on one side of the fenced-in house for fifty-three years. And forty-nine years ago, the Mazza brothers had lived on the other side. The Mazza family had moved to Ozone Park in a period when Italians started to settle the neighbourhood, decamping from Brooklyn. The oldest brother was a bit of a delinquent, and he stole a lot of stuff from around the neighbourhood, especially from his next-door neighbours, an Irish couple with a herd of grown-up kids. He'd wait until no one was around and then just jump the fence and take whatever he wanted. One day, he stole a guitar left on the front porch. Another time, some garden tools went missing from the locked shed. Everyone on the street was sure it was him, but no one could prove it.

Anyway, one day, the neighbours came home to find he'd actually gotten inside the house. And the rent, carefully hidden under a drawer, was gone. Again, they couldn't prove it. But desperate to protect what little they had, the owner gathered up saplings from the woods where the racecourse is now and put up this fence.

Prim pressed her hand against the worn wood, staring up at it.

The old man gestured down the side of the house. "It goes all the way round."

"Did it work?" I asked.

"Well, he didn't rob this family anymore." He chuckled. "The rest of the neighbourhood had to put up with it for a few more years, though."

The thieving only stopped when the Mazza family moved a few blocks away.

But wait, the story's not over yet.

The neighbours would still hear about the Mazza brothers, so quick was gossip to move around the Italian network. Eventually the boy left his petty neighbourhood thieving days and moved on to the more serious work of robberies. He even enlisted one of his brothers. They started robbing shops at night up on Atlantic Avenue.

Years later, a friend of the old guy, who owned a little antiques store in Centreville, kept getting burgled. The police didn't do much, so the shop owner's solution was to wait each night, armed, ready to scare the burglars off. One night they finally came, and the owner got out of the car and burst through his own front door. One of them tried to run off with some money in his hand. He ran for the door, and the owner, thinking the man was coming right for him, fired his gun. The robber died. Guess who he was? Of course, the younger Mazza brother. The oldest went to prison for six years.

"Wow," Prim said. "That is nuts."

The old guy nodded. His nod told me he'd repeated that story a ton of times and knew it was the best he had. It was hard to get him to stop talking after that. As he chatted, gesticulating and going on segues, I itched to take his photo but didn't want to interrupt to ask. I contemplated taking a shot of the fence, but I already knew the image was nothing much without the story. We were saved when another old guy turned up in a van, shouting out the window in Italian. We said our goodbyes and made our escape.

I took one last look back at the fence. "Imagine living somewhere so long you have a story like that to tell?"

"Crazy." Prim plucked at my jacket sleeve, leading me down yet another street.

Later, we stopped for lunch at a bakery called Little Guyana. I had to look on my phone to find out where Guyana was on a map.

"What, you've never heard of it?" Prim asked. "Jonestown? Death by Kool-Aid?"

I shook my head. None of it meant a single thing to me.

Prim bit into her roll and gleefully told me about this famous cult leader who convinced a whole bunch of people to commit suicide by drinking poisoned cordial. Nearly a thousand of them. Voluntarily. Like, as in parents who gave it to their own kids. Isn't that insane? Every time I thought the world couldn't be any weirder, someone—usually Prim—told me something like this.

"Imagine killing your own kid," I said.

Prim just shook her head like she wasn't even going to try to imagine it.

"Do you want to have kids?" I couldn't exactly imagine Prim as the mum type.

"Dunno. Doubt it." She swiped some crumbs from her mouth with her jacket sleeve and stared around her as if that was the most boring topic in the world. I guess I got my answer.

We sat there and ate as the Ozone Park world went by. Guys about our age slouched past, giving us those sideways *I'm checking you out, but I'm not really* looks. Old ladies pushed shopping carts, giving us suspicious glances. Prim finished her roll and wiped her hands free of crumbs. "You know, my dad lives a few streets from here. That way." She pointed up the street.

I stopped chewing. "What?" Welcome to the second Prim revelation for the day.

She just shrugged and stared at some kids trying to leapfrog a pole outside the subway stop.

"I thought you said he moved away. Like, far away."

"He did. The other side of Queens is pretty far, you know." She gave me a teeny lip curl of a smile.

"Yeah, but I thought…" I don't know what I thought.

"It's no big deal, Zel. I was just telling you."

It is a big deal, I wanted to say. But saying it wouldn't make it so for Prim. "Does he live alone?"

"Nah, he's got a girlfriend. And she's got a couple of kids, apparently. I've never met them."

"Is that weird?"

She leaned forward, her elbows on her knees, and scrunched the paper bag into a tighter ball. Finally she shook her head. "You know what? I know I'm *supposed* to care. I know that if this were a book or a movie, I'd feel all tortured that my dad could be really close by and that he has another family and that I haven't seen him this year or most of last. But I just don't care." She tossed the balled-up bag at a bin but missed. Clicking her tongue, she went over and put it in. Then she turned back, giving me this look I'd never seen from her before. She folded her arms over her chest. "See, I keep waiting to care, because I know I'm supposed to. But I just don't. And I know it's weird."

She kept looking at me like she was waiting for me to agree that there was something wrong with her. But I had no idea what to say. I wanted to tell her that this kind of feeling was not just in books or movies, that it was real and possible and that I knew *I'd* feel it. I know I'd be messed up if my dad had a new wife and kid. But who was I to tell her what was the right thing to feel? Or not feel?

"Maybe it's a good thing?" I suggested.

She gave me a nod, but I knew she thought I'd missed the point. I hadn't. I just didn't know what to tell her or how to explain why she was numb to this when everything pointed to the fact that she shouldn't be.

We kept walking through the neighbourhood, looking at the identical houses with their different gardens, everyone's attempt at finding uniqueness in a neighbourhood of conformity. Planes roared past, on the way to JFK Airport on the other side of the freeway.

Prim was quiet after that lunchtime conversation. So was I. I felt guilty.

I felt better when Prim stopped to laugh and point at a collection of garden gnomes in the centre of a narrow strip of lawn. There was a small army of them gathered around a bird bath. I was taking a photo when the voice called out to us.

"Don't even think about trying to steal 'em."

A man and woman sat on their porch, rugged up in big jackets and scarves as they basked in the flimsy late-afternoon sun, guarding their gnomes.

"People steal them?" I pulled a face. What was with Ozone Park?

The woman nodded, her chin disappearing into her neck. "They sure do." She counted off on her fingers. "I lost eight this year."

"But she ain't gonna lose no more." The man, so big that his jacket looked like a bedspread, got up and shuffled down to the lawn. He pushed at one of the gnomes with his foot. "Cemented 'em, didn't I?"

Prim laughed, loud and hard. "Good idea." She nudged me. "There's lot of sticky fingers in this neighbourhood."

We told them about the fence we saw. They loved the story. We chatted to them for a while after that. He was a retired policeman, and she worked at a hospital. He'd lived in Ozone Park since he was born, and she was from Queens too. It was so crazy how much talking we'd been doing with people that day. I mean, you just don't do that in New York. We even told them about the subway project. They were really excited by the idea, asking us about the places we'd been. And you know what was crazy? They'd only been to a couple of places we mentioned. Me, a kid from the other side of the world, had seen more of their city than they had. And that's when I realised that this place was so big you could live your whole life in just one borough without ever seeing the rest. New York was a universe of its own.

On the train home, Prim tucked her hair behind her ears and gave me a wide-eyed smile. "That was amazing."

I smiled and nodded. That was one of the things I loved about Prim and me together, the way we were both so fascinated by these stories and these worlds and the unexpected things we found. We felt like we were these intrepid world explorers.

But I also felt uneasy. And when I got home to the apartment, I couldn't stop thinking about these unsettling Prim terrains I'd been privy to—things that weakened her, rendered her more vulnerable. Made my worship less worship-able. At the same time, those things I learned about her made me glad that I was her friend, even if maybe I wanted more, because I had a feeling I was the only person in the world who knew these things about her. And that suddenly felt like an awesome responsibility.

CHAPTER 20

I remember that moment, Prim talking about her dad, when I find myself having a near-identical conversation with Stella. We're traipsing down the street, hot chocolates warming our hands. It's finally feeling a little cold. Cold for Sydney, anyway.

"I *know*." Stella's on her phone, talking to her mother. I'm guessing from the conversation that it's something about Ollie's arrangements for the night.

I run a hand over my camera bag, checking it's secure. It's a force of habit. Ever since Mum and Dad bought it for my fifteenth birthday, it's been my most precious possession. I've spent the last hour photographing Stella dancing, until we got kicked out of the studio by another kiddie dance class. It was hard to stop, actually. I was getting so many great shots.

If I thought Stella was amazing after watching that one-minute dance with the boys last week, now, after an hour in the studio of watching her warm up and then let herself go, I'm convinced she's incredible. I can't wait to get to my photography class next week and develop the negatives.

Stella stops in the middle of the footpath, glaring at whatever's being said on the other end of the phone. "But I was going to go to the movies this afternoon with Ashani." She tucks her loose hair behind her ears and starts walking again. I'd asked her to take it out while we were in the studio. I'd wanted the flow of her loose hair to add to the sense of movement I was trying to capture.

Stella sighs loudly. "Okay, I'll do it. Bye, Mum." She hangs up. I watch her frown as shoves her phone in her pocket, wondering if I should ask.

She turns to me and gives me a shadow of a smile. "Sorry. Annoying family stuff."

"Your little brother?"

She nods. "We're all supposed to take turns looking after him when Mum has to work, but my brothers and sister are kind of scatty, and they forget they have things on. And it's always me picking up the slack."

"Are the others younger or older?"

"All older except Ollie."

"And your dad?"

"Lives in Queensland. They divorced when Ollie was little. He's got another family now."

"Is that okay?" I flinch. "And is it okay to ask that?"

She shrugs. "It's not great. I don't really see him. He used to send us over for school holidays, but between dance and my brothers' sport stuff and uni, we're all too busy to go regularly. Now we see him maybe once a year. And when we do, it's *super* awkward and depressing."

That's when I remember Prim that day in Ozone Park. Her revelation that she didn't care. Because Stella's answer was the usual kind of response I would have expected from someone.

Stella turns to me and smiles. "And yes, it's okay to ask."

"Good."

"What about your parents?"

"Disgustingly together."

"That's great."

We hit a busy section of footpath and have to weave single file among the café crowds. I follow Stella's slender back and think covetously of the photos in my camera again. As we emerge from the crush, Stella's phone starts to ring. She plucks it from her pocket, stares at the screen, and answers it, frowning. "I know," she says straight away, clearly not even waiting for the other person to answer. She waits another few seconds, frowns, and says, "I *know*" again, sounding kind of angry. She hangs up and turns to me, holding up her hands and dropping them at her sides, frowning. "I have to go."

I nod. Of course. She always has to go. She throws her coffee cup in the bin, gives me an eye roll, and jumps on her bike. And once again, I'm on Bakers Road, watching her fly away. And this is the first time I find myself wishing she'd stayed.

Have you ever felt compelled to figure someone out? That's how I feel about Stella. She veers so confusingly between friendly and indifferent. Today she acted like we've been friends forever. But last time I saw her, with the others at lunchtime yesterday, she barely acknowledged me. I feel like there's this push and pull within her, and you never know which part you are going to get.

I don't totally get her, but I'm completely intrigued by her at the same time.

CHAPTER 21

I guess Prim got my letter. I'm mucking around online when she suddenly appears in chat. I nearly fall off the kitchen counter, I'm so stunned to see her name.

I need to talk to you.

Part of me would love to write, in all caps, *THAT'S WHAT I'VE BEEN SAYING FOR MONTHS*, but instead, I take in a deep breath and type, *Ok.*

Skype on Sunday afternoon? Four thirty your time?

Sure.

And then she's gone.

And suddenly the thing I've wished for all these months becomes the thing I'm dreading. What will she say?

Then, in the spirit of full digital overload, I'm still blinking at the screen, wondering if that exchange really did happen, when my phone beeps on the bench.

It's Antony.

Dress rehearsal at six at my place.

I drag in a deep breath. I'll just have to wait until tomorrow to find out what Prim wants to say. Right now I need to perfect my montage.

But when I drop down from the bench, my legs feel like they've been on a boat for the last ten hours. How the hell am I going to get through the next twenty-four?

~ ~ ~

It wasn't long after that day with Prim in Ozone Park that Mum and Dad told me we'd be leaving New York for Sydney. They told me there was a chance we'd be coming back after Dad finished the Sydney job, but they weren't really sure.

I was both happy and heartbroken. I was happy for Dad. I was. And I knew this was coming at some point; we'd been there for ten months. We were never supposed to be staying in New York forever. But I'd thought we'd have the full year at least. And I'd always thought that when we returned that we'd go back to Canberra. So I was doubly upset when I found out his new job was in Sydney. I didn't want to get used to living in another place again. And of course I didn't want to leave Prim.

We were so close to finishing the subway project. It was hard to believe, but when I looked at the map I'd stuck to the wall of my tiny New York room, with all the lines we'd done already blacked out, I could see it. We were so close. Close enough to finish it.

I didn't tell Prim I was leaving until our next trip. That was when I finally drew Coney Island. I'd seen photos of the boardwalk and the old fun fair and had always wanted to go. Prim thought Coney Island was a big fat cliché, with its amusement park and hot dog-eating contests and chintzy souvenirs, but I didn't care.

It was another one of those icy but sunny days. All the attractions on the boardwalk were closed for winter. It was quiet except for the sound of waves and the sounds of gulls occasionally flying overhead. The only people around were retirees sunning themselves on benches, wrapped in thick coats.

We wrapped our scarves around our necks and the bottoms of our faces and braved the length of the boardwalk. Even though it was freezing, I loved breathing in that sharp sea air. In New York, you hardly ever feel like you're breathing in air that hasn't been breathed or polluted by someone else first. And you definitely never get to feel that sense of space unless you're by the ocean. It reminds you that another world continues beyond it.

I didn't think Coney Island was boring. Not at all. I didn't think Prim did either, once we got there. I could tell she was into it as I watched her tip her face up to the sky when a flock of birds flew past or cackle at an old couple wearing matching fur top hats. The last few weeks, all our trips had been Manhattan-bound, emerging from the subway into neighbourhoods that didn't have the same distinct character or that sense of the exotic that the borough lines did. But Coney Island had it in spades.

We trudged along the wooden promenade all the way to a place called Brighton Beach, in a neighbourhood known as Little Odessa, we found out. It was like all those busy shopping strips we saw on our trips, jammed tightly under the raised rail line, but instead of all the food stores and groceries being Puerto Rican or Dominican, they were Russian. The strip smelt like baking bread, and maybe it was the time of day, but it felt like everyone on the street but us was over sixty. They pushed shopping carts down the sidewalks, hell-bent on their grocery missions, while Prim and I tried to stay out of their way. We explored the shops and examined packaging on groceries, making wild guesses at their contents. We bought pastries and hot tea and took them back with us to sit at the very end of the pier. We ate with our backs to the wind, leaned up against weather-greyed wood. Prim unfolded her subway map and held it flat against her leg. "You know we only have Canarsie and Rockaway to go, right?" she said.

"Really?" I grabbed the map from her. "There are two Rockaways, aren't there? Where the A line splits? Far Rockaway and Rockaway Park Beach?"

She shrugged. "We can do both of them in a day. We can do all three of them all in a day if we try." She plucked a piece of fetta from her pie and tossed it to a gull. It pecked it up and waited for more. "But then what will we do?" She sounded sad.

I fingered the corner of the map. It was starting to tear at the creases. Prim was determined to keep the same one until we were done. I passed it back to her. "I can't believe it."

"Me either." She slowly folded it up and stuffed it into the front pocket of her knapsack. "Let's do it the week after next. I'm working next week."

"Okay." I hesitated, drawing in a breath. "That's probably good. I'm leaving next month." I think I'd been holding onto this information because I still wasn't one hundred per cent sure how she would react. I wasn't sure if she remembered I was only supposed to be there a year. We never talked about it. And I guess I was stalling because I wasn't sure that she'd really care. And if that was the case,

I didn't really want to know. I knew how I felt about it, and that's what kept the words locked inside me until this moment.

She pulled her windswept hair out of her face and stared at me. "What? Where are you going?"

"Back to Australia."

She just blinked at me for a moment. Then she put her food down and stared at the water, saying nothing. "Are you coming back?" she finally asked.

"I don't know." My throat suddenly started to ache. "It depends on Mum and Dad and their jobs. I have no say in it, really."

A slow nod told me she was listening. Then, for a whole long minute, she was as still as a rock. When she finally turned to me, she still didn't speak. But the look in her eyes told me that this was definitely making her feel something.

"I'm sorry," I whispered.

She just nodded again. And then she did something she's never done. She looped her hands around my upper arm, leaned gently against my side, and stared out at the water. She was so close her hair kept blowing against my cheek. It tickled, but I didn't want to move for fear of breaking this moment. It was the first time I was ever certain that Prim needed me.

I turned my head a little so I could watch her bite her lip and frown at the grey, roiling waves. She'd returned to that vulnerable version of Prim I'd gotten hints of in Ozone Park. And maybe it was because I'd never seen her like that. Maybe it was because I was so overwhelmed that the news that I was leaving made her look like that. Maybe it was the way she was holding onto me. Whatever it was, the moment she turned to meet my eyes, I leaned forward, my heart beating furiously, and kissed that frowning mouth.

It was just for a second. And it used up all the brave I had in me. And when I pulled back, she was wide-eyed and still. I felt instantly sick to my stomach. I had no idea what she was thinking. I just knew from her frozen expression that she was surprised. And my stupid, hungry, big gay heart prayed it was a good kind of surprised.

When she still wouldn't speak, I whispered, "I'll miss you. So much."

She dropped her chin and nodded, and I felt like I watched a hundred half thoughts cross her face in those few seconds before she lifted her gaze to look at me again. When I leaned in to kiss her one more time, she kissed me back.

I want to say that kissing Prim was the most incredible thing that ever happened, that afterwards everything was perfect. That it went the way all those scenarios I had let myself imagine went—where I kissed Prim and she realised she felt the same. But it didn't. She didn't push me away either, though. Just quietly acquiesced. It was *all* so quiet, like we were being gentle with each other.

Afterwards, we didn't hold hands or touch each other again or do any of those things people are supposed to do after they kiss for the first time. Prim didn't even really look at me. And we definitely didn't talk. I put it down to the surprise, to the news that I was going.

We left the boardwalk not long after that, after the silence became too big. I remember feeling like I was bursting with something, with this possibility. But at the same time, I felt so incredibly unsure. We walked to the subway, a few feet of space between us. Prim's hands were jammed in her pockets, her chin dug into her scarf. She was a fortress again.

The train was packed, and we stood silent in the clutch of people, avoiding each other's eyes. Prim got off the train before me. And all she offered at her stop was a quiet "bye" before she disappeared into a crowd of passengers at the door.

As the train took me to Manhattan, I knew I should feel happy. But instead, I just felt like crying. At first, I thought it was because Prim and I had finally got here, a place I never really thought we would, and now I was leaving. But then I started to wonder if it was because what we'd just made already seemed so incredibly, impossibly fragile.

I knew it shouldn't feel like this. So why did it?

Maybe we hadn't just created something together. Maybe I had just ruined something.

CHAPTER 22

I didn't hear from Prim again.

And just like the characters in our book, Far Rockaway was never destined to be a good memory. Life accidentally imitating art didn't feel that good, it turned out.

She didn't answer my messages in the days after Coney Island. I tried calling her, then I tried the two forms of social media Prim deigned to use. I even tried her home phone. Nothing. And I may not have been that experienced, but I knew from every TV show and movie I'd ever seen that when a girl doesn't call you back after you kiss her, something's probably not right.

But still I held out hope. I told myself that maybe she was just upset that I was leaving. I mean, I had taken her by surprise. And she'd been sad that day on the pier, right? She was. Maybe she was busy with school and her job. Maybe she just needed a minute to compute all this.

But the silence became longer and more terrifying, and I started to admit to myself that this was definitely not good. I called her, I messaged her, I even emailed, but I got nothing. And when I still hadn't heard anything a couple of days before our planned Rockaway trip, I was sure. Prim had cut herself off from me. I didn't know exactly why, but I knew it hurt like hell.

As the Rockaway date passed and I began to pack up my New York life, I spent most of my days on my bed, staring at my computer or out the window. Luckily, Mum and Dad just thought it was generalised moving-out of New York misery, because I didn't want to tell them anything. It was too private. And I think maybe I was a little embarrassed.

The weekend before I left, Keeley and Beth took me out for a last trip around Manhattan. We went to a bunch of the tourist spots and then finished the day with a big, obesity-friendly American meal. It was sweet of them, and I did my best to be a pleasant human being, but it was like salt in the wound. All I could think about was that the day had been nowhere near as cool or fun as all those adventures to the unknown corners of New York. And I definitely couldn't tear my mind from the fact that there was a great big black hole of silence where Prim used to be. And it hurt. Bad.

My dad is really into rules for life. He likes to spring them on me at random. For example, the other night when he was making us sandwiches for dinner, he waved a knife in the air and said, "Rule for life, Zel: mayonnaise makes everything better."

I'll admit that his rules for life can be only marginally useful. But sometimes the rule is something more substantial like "Never get a tattoo where the judge can see it" or "Interrogate the obvious". (I'm still not one hundred per cent sure what that one means.) But you never know when you're going to get one about condiments. Either way, it's hard to take them completely seriously. Because in the sixteen years I've been on this planet, Dad has given me at least three thousand rules for life but has never given me a curfew.

Here's a good rule for life: never tell someone you love them unless you're sure they're going to say it back. And an even better rule: Never tell someone you love them right before you're about to move to another country. Because they might not reply. Or you might not be around when they're ready to.

But I am a reckless fool, and that's exactly what I did. I couldn't think of a single other thing to do. I'd called her, I'd messaged, I'd stalked her online. Nothing.

It was the day before we were getting on the plane to Sydney. I couldn't bear leaving without seeing her. I paced my now-empty room, chewed my fingernails to stubs, and checked my phone endlessly. Nothing.

I told my parents I was going to a last photography class (let's put it on record: I think lying to your parents is super crappy, but I was feeling crazy that day) and jumped on the subway to Brooklyn. On the crowded Saturday afternoon train, I was only half-aware of the smell of damp, rain-soaked clothes, and the crush of commuting bodies around me. It was raining heavily when I got to her stop (why was it always raining in her neighbourhood?), and I dashed underneath one shop awning to the other. I went past her work, but she wasn't there. I continued up 4th Avenue to her apartment.

The risk I was taking in doing this didn't hit me until I stood in front of her door. That's when the fear tumbled through me, the way a surf wave hits you from behind, nearly knocking you off your feet. I held my ground, my fingers grasping the paint-chipped doorjamb, and knocked.

When the door opened, I thought for a second I'd knocked at the wrong apartment. And it was only the familiar room behind the tiny woman staring at me that convinced me I was at the right place.

This was Prim's mother? As I tried to muster speech, her eyes narrowed. That suspicious gaze was the only feature on this woman I could connect to Prim. Besides that, I couldn't figure out a single way in which this woman could have produced her. She was small and rounded where Prim was all lank. Her skin was a pale olive while Prim's complexion was pale and youth perfect. Her mouth was pinched where Prim's was wide.

"I'm a friend of Prim's," I stuttered. "Is she home?"

The woman relaxed slightly, loosening her grip on the door. (I'm sure she'd been preparing to slam it in my face if necessary.) And her gaze widened enough that I discovered another of Prim's features she shared with her mother: those almond eyes. The woman nodded and gave in to a small smile. "Sorry, she's not home." I couldn't place her accent, but I'd heard tiny traces of it in Prim when she said certain words.

"Oh," I said. And then I just stood there like an idiot. Because I had no idea where to look next.

"I don't know where she is either, I'm sorry." This time, she did close the door in my face. Not rudely, but quietly.

As I stumbled down the stairs, not quite ready to accept the fact that I'd run out of places to look, it occurred to me how weird it was that her mother didn't know where she was. I remember Prim saying that her mother always demanded to know her location at any given time. The only reason Prim had a mobile phone was so her mother could track her down and check constantly that she was alive.

I froze, horrified. Had Prim gotten her mother to say that she didn't know where she was? Was she actually home and hiding? Did she need to avoid me that badly? I had no way of knowing for sure, but the thought made my stomach hurt.

Tear blind and miserable, I trudged back to the subway, not even bothering to duck the rain this time. I stood on the platform, jaw clenched, frowning into the dark space where the train would be soon. I wasn't just heartbroken. Now I was kind of pissed. Why couldn't she talk to me? Was she really going to let the last five months of friendship just turn into nothing?

By the time I got home and finished the last bits of my packing, the anger was still there. And that's when I did something even more stupid. Right before I turned out my light for the last time in New York, I picked up my phone and messaged her.

I wish you'd let me say goodbye before I leave.

Nothing. And then, because I wanted her to understand and because I needed to fill the silence that immediately followed, I typed another message.

I love you.

I flinched and pressed *send*. Then I burrowed under my covers and willed myself to go to sleep.

CHAPTER 23

On Saturday night, we hold our dress rehearsal. It's not really one, though, given that there are no actual costumes. Stella and the boys wear leggings and T-shirts with their feet bare. We like the combination of everyday clothes with the dance instead of costumes, like they could be anybody and everybody.

I'm finally happy with my photo montage. Just like I planned, I designed it as a progression, starting with images of people standing outside their houses. I got the idea for the opening one night when we were having dinner at Rosa's and one of my uncles was showing Antony and I photos of Nonna and Nonno in front of their first house in Canberra, when they arrived in Australia after the war. They stand there so proudly outside their perfectly manicured front garden, staring at the camera with such solemn expressions. On the internet, I found similar shots to that one and have arranged them in order so that as each image flashes by, the homes people stand in front of are progressively worse: children standing outside slums on city fringes, people in front of tents in refugee camps, and families curled up sleeping at railway stations, waiting for trains to Europe. Then finally, the last shot is of people standing behind fences at Australia's detention centres, followed by a famous news picture of the babies born in detention.

When I first showed Ashani, a smile spread slowly across her face. I'd never seen her smile like that. "That's amazing," she said.

And I have to admit, it felt good. She might rub me the wrong way, but I care what Ashani thinks about this project. The montage works really well with her voice recordings too. Because at first, the images match what the people are describing, all these warm, cosy ideas of home and family, and then the words and pictures start to completely diverge. It's exactly the effect we wanted. It's perfect.

For the dress rehearsal, we've borrowed one of the portable projectors from the school and brought it to Antony's place so we can see how it all works together for the first time. I'm actually excited.

The performance is only three minutes long. I thought it should be longer, but Ashani had insisted it would start to drag. "Short is more forceful," she said.

I see what she means as I watch it all put together in Antony's backyard, the images projected on the walls of his house, the three of them dancing their steps on the concrete below. You just have time to get it, and then it's done, leaving you with just the feelings—hopefully feelings that make you want to do something about what you've seen, Michael says. I hope so too.

When it's finished, Ashani turns her chair around next to me with this huge smile. It's one of those excited, slightly stunned smiles that say *did you see that too?* And I nod and grin back, because I saw exactly what she saw: the piece coming together exactly the way we wanted it to. She holds up a hand, and I slap it.

The others are looking at us expectantly, hands on hips, still catching their breath. We give them the deserved slow clap.

"It's incredible, guys." I sit up. "We've got this."

"Agreed." Ashani taps away on her computer, back to business. "I just want to clean up the sound a touch, make the edits cleaner." I shake my head. This girl doesn't know the meaning of resting on her laurels. She turns to me. "I think our sound and vision is out by a second or half a second. We could overcome the lag by just putting them into one file together."

"Sure," I say, without a hint of my usual Ashani-reactionary sass. I think I've started to realise that she is really great at this stuff and that I should just let her be. Because if she has her way, this show will be perfect. And there's nothing wrong with that, right?

We run through it a couple more times, and then when we're done, no one seems to want to go home. Not even Stella. So instead we hang out in Antony's backyard. I lounge around on a sunbed and breathe in the night air. It smells sweet out here. Antony's long, narrow yard is full of flowers. Rosa loves them. My nonna used to chide her for not growing vegetables like she always did, but Rosa didn't care. She just likes to have flowers all the year round.

I stretch out and play with the long petals of a purple flower drooping by my shoulder and idly watch Stella flop on the sunbed next to me. She tucks her hands behind her head and shuts her eyes while Michael gossips about someone in our Drama class.

You know those blissful moments that come around, rare as hell but magical for that fact? Tonight feels like one of them. It's a still, sweet Sydney night, and the air smells like my aunt's flower jungle. Our performance has come together as perfectly as we can possibly make it, and it's the middle of the weekend. I'm feeling so good I can even manage to tuck away my fears for a minute about talking to Prim tomorrow.

A window next door opens, and the sound of laughter and clattering dishes pours out. Somewhere behind the chatter, I hear the restless sounds of a piano. I'm no classical music fan, but it's perfect for right now. I just lie there, letting the notes wash over me.

Antony goes inside to get us snacks, and Michael stands, pulling Ashani with him. He pulls her into a slow waltz on the gravel, moving to the piano music. Ashani throws her head back and laughs but does it. They turn in slow, formal little circles as the chatter next door gets louder, and the music louder still. Stella and I laugh at the sight of them. Antony comes back outside with some bowls in his hand. He puts them down on the table and laughs too, even though the competition has his girl. It's that kind of night.

Suddenly Stella kicks her legs over her lounge chair. I think she's going to get herself something to eat, but instead she turns to me, her long fingers reaching for mine. "Come on."

"What?"

"Dance."

I shake my head, horrified. "I can't dance."

She smiles wider and shrugs. It's not one of those typical Stella shrugs, where she's cutting things off, closing a conversation with one of her nonresponses. Not this time. She's shrugging to tell me it doesn't matter, that a small thing like not being able to dance shouldn't stop me. And because she never smiles at me like that, all cocky charm, I choose to believe her.

I sigh loudly but let her pull me up. She adjusts her grip on my hand, presses her fingers lightly to my waist, and we slowly begin to swirl around our small patch of gravel. She's right. It doesn't matter if I can't dance, because she can. And I have nothing to do but to respond to the light guiding touch of her finger on my waist. Something about having her so close makes me feel incredibly shy, but happy too. And because I don't know what to do with that feeling, I tuck it away. We both laugh as we turn in circles on our little patch of gravel. Antony claps his hands, guffawing at this small spectacle.

I grin conspiratorially at Stella as Antony cuts in on Michael and Ashani. She gives me a sly smile back and begins to move faster. Even though she's smaller than me, she commands our movements as we spin around on the gravel.

When I nearly trip, I break into giggles again, and Stella pulls me a little closer. She smells good. She smells like… Okay, bear with me, it's not *like* watermelon, but like a scent that gives you the same sensation as watermelon. It's light and fresh and just a little fragile.

It's all ridiculous but fun, fun because we're all doing it. That kind of hilarity and abandon where everyone is doing something they'd never usually do. Suddenly something completely stupid seems like the only thing in the world you should do.

We dance for ages, taking turns to cut in on each other. I even take a turn with Antony, and we laugh loud and hard, because we've never danced together, never even been this close to each other in our lives. He's so formal and dignified, like an old-fashioned gentleman. But he's also a terrible slow dancer, and he makes me even clumsier. I submit to his halting waltz and watch Michael twirl Stella. Secretly I wish I was still moving under her silent, graceful tuition. But before we can all change partners again, the window next door closes, and the music becomes a muted thing, too soft for our little impromptu ball.

Later, Stella and I walk home together, the loose, light mood of this night still cloaking us. She tells me stories about her old ballet recitals. She giggles and cracks jokes as she recalls little girls falling off stages, prop malfunctions, kids wetting their pants in the wings. I laugh and beg for more and wish she was always like this.

Chapter 24

Have you ever seen one of those YouTube videos, like that famous one by that poor girl who'd been bullied—the one where she was too scared to speak her story so she held up cards, one by one, with her story written on them? That's what Prim did to me.

At four thirty, I sit in Dad's workroom, where the internet is always best, and wait, my stomach clenched into this tight knot. I've brushed my hair, reapplied my eyeliner and mascara, and generally tried to look decent, but even I can see the taut lines of fear between my eyebrows when I check my reflection.

Finally the call comes through. I haul in a breath and accept it. And a few seconds later, there is Prim on my screen. Although I can barely concentrate over the drumroll of my heart, the first thing I notice is her haircut. She has bangs now, the kind that fall right on her brow, framing those alien brown eyes. Now she really looks like a model. The second thing I realise is that she must have a computer, because she's sitting on her bed with her hands free. I can see Violet curled up behind her.

It takes a second to remember how to breathe, I'm so terrified. Finally, I let out a soft "hi".

Her mouth moves in the direction of a smile but doesn't quite get there. I wait for her to speak, but instead she crosses her legs on the bed and lifts up a large notepad with black text scrawled on it. I lean in closer, trying to make it out. As I peer at it, she moves the pad closer, and the text comes into focus, dominating the screen.

> I have to tell you these things, but I don't know
> how to say them out loud.

Even while I'm feeling the first flickers of dread, I realise that I've never seen Prim's handwriting before. I've seen her doodles, little pictures scribbled on the edge of subway maps or on newspapers during long train rides, but never her writing. It's round and lopsided like a child's.

Her eyes bore into me over the edge of the notepad, and I know they're willing me to respond. In the spirit of this silence, I just nod. Her shoulders lift and fall on either side of the pad as she draws in a breath, and then she slowly turns the page.

> First thing, I do love you.
> But not like that.

I grip the sides of my laptop, feeling the instant prick of tears.
She turns another page.

> You're the best friend I've ever had.

And another.

> And I kissed you back because I knew you liked
> me that way, and I didn't want to lose you.

The clench in my stomach loosens, and my guts start to swim instead. Had I been that obvious? My face begins to burn, and I stare at my hands clenched in my lap so I won't have to look at her.

When I lift my eyes, she turns the page again immediately.

> And at first, I thought if that was the way I had to
> keep you, I would do it.
> But I knew it wasn't fair.

Even though it almost physically hurts, I bring myself to meet her eye and nod so she knows I'm hearing—well, reading—what she has to say. I owe her that at least.

Sorrow slides to shame. Shame that she felt like she had to kiss me back to keep me. Did I really make her feel like that? Before I can think of what to possibly say, she turns another page.

> The thing is, I don't feel that way about anybody.

She stares at me over the top of the paper as she turns the page again. She doesn't blink.

> It's like there's this gap between me and nearly everyone else.
> I think there's something wrong with me.

I can see tears in her eyes. I realise I have never seen Prim even close to crying. It feels like everything that is horrible and strange. I hold her gaze but say nothing. Because what do you say to that? I feel like I've been passed a huge, heavy weight. My guilt, yes, but part of it is sadness for Prim. For whatever these fears are that she's trying to articulate to me.

> I keep waiting to feel something, but it never happens. And I know it's not normal.

I shake my head furiously, and I go to tell her that she's okay, but she turns the page again. I stop to read as she flips one page after the other, each with just one line on them.

> But the one thing I feel normal about is you.

> You're my favourite person. My best friend.

> I miss you. I miss talking to you. I miss exploring the world with you.

> And I'm so sorry I don't feel more than that.

She drops the notepad on the bed in front of her, swipes at a stray tear with her sleeve, and stares at the bedcovers.

And that fallen tear makes me suddenly feel like there's no air left in the room. I go to tell her that I'm sorry too, but she leans toward the computer, and then suddenly she's gone.

~ ~ ~

I'm still sitting there riding the aftershocks of that brutal little call when Dad comes home. He's about to fly to Canberra to source some old patterns or something. He rushes in, shoving things into a bag. Finally, as he zips his laptop into its case, he spots me.

"What's this pile of misery I see before me?" he jokes as he sits down next to me and runs a hand over my hair.

I just give him a this is serious look and wipe my eyes with the back of my hands.

"Oh, hey," he says, softer this time. "Seriously, kiddo. Are you okay?"

And because it's still so raw and I don't know who else in the world I could possibly talk to about this stuff, I tell him. I need someone to make sense of this for me.

I haltingly tell him about Prim and me and a little bit about what happened at Coney Island and after. Then I tell him about what she just said to me. "How do things become such a mess?" I'm crying again. Ugly sobs I'm glad no one else is around to see.

"Surprisingly easily at your age." He wraps his arm around my shoulder and squeezes me, and even though I am sixteen and not six, it's kind of nice to have the comfort of a cuddle from Dad. It also makes me cry more.

"Well, I can't wait to get older, then." I rest my head on his shoulder, breathing in that comforting Dad scent of aftershave and man smell.

"I always thought there might have been something between you two, but you never said, and I wanted to respect your privacy."

"Well, it turns out there was nothing there anyway." I chew on a fingernail, a habit I got rid of years ago. I shrug. "I'll get over it."

"Just because your feelings weren't reciprocated doesn't mean they didn't exist or weren't valid," he says.

I nod, even though I'm not one hundred per cent sure I believe him.

He rubs a hand over my hair again. "And you'll feel better about it one day, I promise. It just takes a while."

"It's not just about me, though." My finger is still jammed in my mouth. "I don't know if Prim's okay. The stuff she said about not feeling normal, about not connecting to people, it's freaking her out." I tell him about what she said to me in Ozone Park, about how she didn't care about her dad leaving. "That *isn't* normal, is it?"

He shakes his head. "I don't know, hon. I don't know her." He taps his wedding band against his front tooth, this thing he always does when he's thinking hard. "It might just be that she's closed herself off to those feelings so tightly. People do that for self-protection sometimes when their trust has been broken enough. And maybe now she's having trouble accessing them."

I nod. That's another thing I love about Dad. He talks to me like I'm a grown-up. He takes me seriously, and he believes my feelings are real. "And what she was saying about not liking anybody?" He turns to face me. "It could be part of the whole being closed off to feelings thing. And maybe it will change when she learns to trust. Then there are some people who have difficulty feeling romantic or sexual love toward others. It just doesn't happen to them."

"I'd hate that." And then I blush hard, because I remember that I'm saying this to my father.

"Of course you would." He chuckles. "We're Italian. Not feeling love would kill us."

I shake my head and grin at him. "You're such a cliché."

"There's a reason things become clichés. Anyway, it worries me that she's distressed about all this."

I nod. Poor Prim. "It worries me too."

"Of course it does."

"Dad, I don't want her to feel like that."

"No one wants anyone to feel like that." He squeezes my shoulder again. "That girl needs you."

I feel like I'm about to be consumed by another wave of misery. "But she doesn't want me."

"No, maybe not like that. But she does need you as her friend, or she wouldn't be telling you this. I get the feeling she's not the kind of girl to share much, right?"

I eke out a smile. "Definitely not."

"Well, I'm not just saying this because you're my daughter." He chuckles quietly. "Okay, well, I am saying this because you're my daughter and I know you so well. You're a good person, and you're the kind of person even difficult people like because you make them feel *good*. You're interested, and you don't let a little reticence stop you. I remember when you were younger, you were the only one who could get Antony to play and be a kid and talk. Your nonno said he nearly had a heart attack when he looked out the window and saw Antony laughing hysterically at something you were doing."

I smile. It did used to be my life mission to crack Antony up.

"Anyway, even if you're a bit broken-hearted right now, I hope you can still be her friend. Because if you are one of the only people she feels she can connect with at this point in her life, then she *needs* you."

I breathe out a loud sigh and nod. I already know that. I do. But I have to figure out *how* I can do that. How I can carry my sadness and hers. How we can find a normal again.

Chapter 25

On Monday morning, I tell Mum I'm sick. Talking to Dad yesterday helped, definitely, but I still feel miserable. I can't stop feeling awful about the fact that I might have pressured Prim into something. Every time I think about that, I squeeze my eyes shut and pull the sheets over my head, trying to block out the thought. That's not really how you want your first proper romantic kiss to go, is it? Put it this way: it's definitely a kick to the butt of my self-confidence. And I hate what it might have done to Prim's too. And now I want to shrivel into a tiny non-existent ball for a week, or however long it takes for the feeling to go away.

Of course I'm not sick, but I just can't face school. Luckily, Mum chooses to believe me. I think I get away with it partly because I look like crap from the crying and the not sleeping but also because I've never faked a sick day in my life. Sure, maybe I've milked a flu a day longer than I needed to a couple of times, but I've never outright lied to get out of going to school.

And lucky for me, Mum doesn't know that today is the day we're supposed to perform our Drama project in class. Not that it matters. There's nothing I actually *need* to do during the performance. Ashani presses *play* and the others dance. My bit's already done. Still, for the hour after Mum leaves for work, after telling me to drink water and heat soup for lunch, I veer wildly between waves of sadness and waves of guilt.

And I'm cresting one of the guilt waves when the doorbell rings.

I don't know why I answer it. Really, I don't. I should just stay in bed and text later. But I guess I'm not that great at this pulling a sickie stuff. So I yank a hoodie over my sleep-sweaty body and trudge to the front door.

It's Stella. And she's actually smiling. "Hey. Want to grab hot chocolate on the way?"

"Can't. I'm sick."

"What's wrong?"

"I don't know. A flu or something." I shrug and lean on the doorjamb, hoping my tear-blurred sleep has produced a sickly enough pallor to pass me.

She tips her head to one side, staring at me.

I need it to stop. "Hang on a sec." I rush to my bedroom and grab the USB with the slideshow on it. I'm ninety-nine per cent sure Ashani's already got a copy of it, but I just have to remove myself from the silent Stella scrutiny for a moment. I thrust it into her hand. "Here. Ashani knows what to do."

She looks at the tiny plastic rectangle in her palm and then back at me. I can't read her expression, but I'm pretty sure there are no happy, Zel-loving thoughts in there.

"I'm really sorry," I mumble. "And break a leg."

"Okay, well, feel better," she finally says and turns and dashes down the front stairs.

I close the door, let out a breath, and vow not to open the door or answer a phone for the rest of the day. Or maybe my life.

I spend the day in bed, trying to think of nothing. But of course, nothing keeps being interrupted by sad Prim thoughts, Drama guilt, and non-specific misery. Part of me wants to hate Prim for what she did. For rejecting me by ignoring me for all those months. But another part of me just wants to talk to her all over again, to try to make her feel better.

The Drama guilt gets worse in the afternoon of course, right around the time class starts. I keep imagining them doing the show and then forcing myself not to think about it. Instead I try to watch a show in bed, but really, I'm just staring at a moving screen.

Later, when Mum gets home, I pretend to be half-asleep and tell her I'm not hungry. If I eat dinner with her, she'll start asking questions. And I don't want to answer them. I just need to process this on my own. She leaves me alone. I get the feeling Dad might have told her something.

That night, Stella emails me. Swallowing hard, I open it. The message is blank, but there's a file attached. It's a video of the performance. I watch it even though the remorse is awful and the video quality worse. But even through the fuzz and crappy sound, I can see it is nearly as great as we wanted it to be. When

Stella and the boys stop dancing, the class breaks into applause. I smile. We did it. Well, they did it.

~ ~ ~

I spend one more day at home, playing out my sickness a bit longer, buying myself some time so I don't look like some kind of zombie when I get back to school. But instead of just moping, my guilty conscience convinces me to treat the day like my own personal study hall, catching up on a Psych project I've neglected for Drama and writing up last week's Bio lab report. Basically I work very hard at not thinking.

In the afternoon, I go through a series of contact sheets from the subway project. Trips to Eastchester and Van Cortlandt Park. It's hard to look at them after this thing with Prim, but I make myself. I *need* to find my concept for this project. And it's not even about Stedman now, it's about me. I actually want to find something now that pulls my photos together for the project. If I can't feel good about my love life or my best friend, then I want to at least feel good about my artwork. But it just isn't coming today. And there's only so long you can stare blankly at a contact sheet before you go cross-eyed and even blanker. I give up and turn to my English essay.

By Wednesday, I'm actually dying to get back to school. That's how sick of myself I am. I'm glad I don't have Drama class, though. I don't know if I can face the others. Or Stella's stare. Even Ashani was sympathetic about me being sick, but I still feel like I've let them down. My guilt makes me want to avoid them, but I see Michael in the hall first thing in the morning. Well, he sees me, because I'm too busy worrying about what to do about Prim to notice anything going on in my actual life.

"Zel!" he bellows. He plants himself right in front of me, stopping me in my tracks. He brings his face in closer, peering, and then throws arms out. "You look like you need a hug." Next thing I know, he's enfolding me in the biggest bear hug I've endured in a while. And because I'm feeling so crappy and because he's such a sweetheart, I just bury my face in his thick windcheater, which smells comfortingly like wool wash, and give in. He only lets me go as the bell rings for class. "Whatever's making you look like that this morning, it'll get better. I promise."

I slap his arm, grateful for the brotherly concern. "Thanks, Michael. I'll see you."

He gives me a wave and leaves for his class. I head to mine feeling better, if only for a minute.

First two periods, I have Art. And lucky me, we're allowed to work on our assignments. I sit next to Jason, my chin in my hand, and stare blankly at the same contact sheets I stared blankly at yesterday. Yay for progress.

He nudges me. "Cheer up, would you?"

"Trying."

"Want to talk about it?"

"Definitely not."

"Righto. Got it." His smile is one part Jason default smart-ass and one part genuine sympathy. "Let me know if you change your mind."

"Sure."

He goes back to his computer, and I go back to alternating between gazing futilely at my photos and staring out the window at a cluster of girls sitting behind some bushes near the fitness centre. They're in shorts, so I guess they're skipping PE. I wonder if the twits know how easily they can be seen from here? Not exactly stealth.

Bored, I check out what Jason's doing. On his screen is footage of a wave moving in, hitting rocks, breaking up, and retreating again. It plays over and over, and I can't tell if they are different waves or if he's got it on some sort of loop. I ask him.

"Awesome." He rubs his hand together. "That's *exactly* what I want people to ask."

"Glad you're having a good day." I fight the urge to put my chin on the table. I might be getting away with slacking, but I'm pretty sure Stedman will spot that in seconds. Besides, I remind myself, I don't have time for wallowing. This project's due in a few weeks.

I take a deep, bracing breath and force myself to look at all the photos I've selected. So far, I've chosen them for no other reason than that they're the best ones. I stare first at the one of the blurred figures moving in and out of shops in Astoria, then at the one with the plane flying over the crowds in Flushing. My gaze moves over others: a clump of a jogger's feet on the wet paths of Central Park, a group of kids jumping for a thrown ball at the same time, a long line of commuters disappearing into the subway in identical suits. And I don't know if it's just the right time or it was there all along, but suddenly, *finally*, my depressed, traumatised brain makes way for a tiny epiphany. I see what glues them together. How did something so obvious take so long to appear?

And like she has some sort of telepathy, Stedman chooses that minute to appear at the table. "Hello, you two."

I don't even answer her greeting. I just point at the pictures. "It's movement. It's the constant, relentless movement."

She looks down at the pictures and nods, as if immediately catching on. "Go on."

I stare at them all one by one again, taking my time. They look different now, just by me recognising this parallel between them all. "That's what all the ones I like seem to show about the city." I can feel Jason next to me, leaning in, looking. He smiles and nods, and I know I'm onto something. "And it's like everyone is constantly going somewhere, but at the same time, they're going nowhere. They're still just in this one city, this one neighbourhood, this one dot on a map. Maybe I can use a map to show that somehow…" I falter then, the rest of that thought evading me for now. But it's a seed of an idea.

And Stedman must think so too because she gives me what I never thought I'd see from her: she taps the table and smiles. "Good. Keep going." Then she moves on to the next table.

I turn to Jason, hand up, mouth wide. "That's *it*?"

He just chuckles and shrugs.

"After all that agony and torture? After all that nagging? That's all I get?"

"It's Stedman, man. Take it as high praise."

"I know." I put my cheek down on the desk. "But I feel like I just went through labour, and she gives me 'Good, keep going.' Pfft."

He pats my hand. "Don't look to others," he says, all preachy and patronising. "You should let the art be the reward."

"Shut up, you." But I can't help smiling.

Chapter 26

On Thursday night I'm walking up Bakers Road, coming back from my photography class. It's the first day I feel like I'm getting a bit closer to normal. Not knowing what to do or feel about Prim is still on me like a weight, but finally having a concept for my art project feels pretty damn good.

I'm also feeling better because in my backpack, nestled between two text books, is a contact sheet with Stella's dance photos. And even though I haven't looked at them properly, I have a feeling they're going to be good. I've brought them home because I wanted to look at them in my own time, not with Miriam and Wayne, my senior citizen photography pals, breathing over my shoulder, making their comments.

This is my favourite part of photography, the moment before you see the full result. You get to savour the feeling of maybe having created something magical before you see it, before your inner critic kicks in and you start thinking how you could have done something better. In this in-between time, you get to hold onto the hope that you've done something that translates what you saw through the lens into an image. Trust me, it's harder than it sounds.

Part of the pressure of wanting these ones to work out is because I have to show them to Stella. And what if they're no good and I wasted her time? Or what if I made her think I was worthy of trying to capture what she does on film and I'm really not? As you can see, we're not exactly working with high-confidence Zel today.

It's weird. It's like I conjured her. Because as I pass the bus stop and the crowd of schoolkids and people heading home from work thins, I see her standing on the side of the footpath ahead of me up the hill. There's no mistaking that hair or that posture. There's a little boy by her side in a dark-blue school uniform, and a girl is talking to her, someone I vaguely recognise from school.

I slow down and watch from a distance. I know it's creepy, but I'm curious to see her interact with someone outside our Drama group. And curious about her brother too. He doesn't seem to be paying any attention to Stella and the girl. He's standing there, staring at the passing cars, pointing and saying something neither of them is listening to.

He looks happier than Stella, though. She's got her arms crossed over her chest, and she's staring at the girl like she's not in the least bit interested in what she has to say. This is not your typical impassive Stella either. This is pointed non-engagement. Whoa, burn. Well, it would be if the girl wasn't totally oblivious to it, chatting and gesticulating away.

The minute she stops talking, Stella says what can't have been more than one word in response. Then she puts her hand on her brother's shoulder and steers him away. The girl says something to him and smiles and waves, but he doesn't react at all. They move off up the hill while the girl turns and walks the hill towards me.

She's tall and rangy with long blonde hair. I recognise her. She's in the year above me. I remember when she and a guy got up at school assembly once and talked about a charity project the Year 11 kids are doing. She looks pretty relaxed after what looked to me like a total brush-off. Maybe she doesn't care. She passes me with a brief *maybe I know you* smile.

I give her a polite smile back and watch Stella and her brother walk downhill. I quicken my step until I eventually catch up with them halfway up the hill to our street.

"Hey," I puff, coming up behind her.

Stella jumps and turns, frowning. And she doesn't exactly cheer up when she sees it's me either. But I like to think I'm used to the constant run of Stella hot and cold by now. Sometimes you just have to give her a minute to warm up.

"Hey," she says in that monotone of hers. I haven't heard that in a while.

I ignore it. "How are you?"

She shrugs. The little boy glances at me and then goes back to running his hand along a brick fence. "That's my little brother, Ollie."

"Hi," I say. He doesn't even turn. The next fence is metal, and he keeps running his hands along it, his fingers bouncing loudly off the railings.

Stella steps over and clasps his wrist. "Hey, be gentle," she tells him in a soft voice. "Don't hurt your hand."

He shakes her off but does as he's told, touching the bars more gently. She turns back to me. "Don't be offended if he ignores you."

"I won't." I mean, Stella's got me pretty well trained in that department. If I'd been offended by her ignoring me, I certainly wouldn't be walking here with her with a sheet full of photos in my backpack of her dancing, would I?

But something tells me that right now is not the moment for Zelda the smart-ass. I quicken my pace to keep up with her. "I was just coming home from photography class."

She nods.

"And I saw you talking to that girl from school." She doesn't respond, so I forge on with my ramble. "She's in Year 11, right?"

She gives me the barest nod, and I decide to change the subject. Because she's *clearly* not into that one.

"So, how was your day?"

She just shrugs. Seriously, I know teenagers are supposed to have the art of the shrug down, but Stella's the queen. It's both fascinating and highly irritating. Right now, though, it's definitely erring on the side of irritating. Why does it always feel like two steps forward, one step back with her? One day you feel like you're getting closer to her, and the next she's like this.

I have one last conversation attempt in me. "Hey, guess what I've got in my bag?"

She lets out a little breath, like it's annoying to even maintain her minimal upkeep on this conversation. "What?"

I stop walking, clicking my tongue loudly. I'm done. "Well, I'm sorry to bother you. I was just going to tell you that I've developed the photos and I have them here." I use my best I'm-sounding-light-but-I'm-really-actually-pissed tone. "But I can see you're having a lot of difficulty mustering a crap about anything but yourself right now, so I guess I'll leave you to it." I take off. And I don't look back to see her reaction. I'm too pissed. Hurt, even. No one should have to work this hard at being someone's friend.

~ ~ ~

That night, I'm lying on the couch next to Dad, watching some cooking reality fiasco. Dad's addicted to these shows. Sometimes I wish he'd cook more than he watches other people do it, though. He's really good when you actually get him in the kitchen, but he hardly ever has the time to cook proper meals. Though to be fair, Mum and I don't exactly do much in that department either. Mum's area of expertise is rattling the number for the local Thai and Japanese off by heart. Mine's changing up dressings on a chicken salad.

This cooking show is particularly stupid. All these people sitting around insulting each other's culinary skills. Thrilling stuff. I pick up my phone and see a message from Stella I didn't hear come in earlier.

> *I'm really, really sorry about today. I was in a terrible mood. I shouldn't have taken it out on you.*

Wow. Was not expecting that. I'm no more clued into the mysteries of Stella than I was earlier, but at least it's an apology, right? And because I'm not the grudge-holding kind, I quickly type a reply.

> *It's ok. Bad day?*

There's no response, but her sudden telecommunications appearance does remind me of the pictures in my bag. I slap Dad's knee as the commercials end. "Sorry, Papa, you're on your own."

I go hunt down my bag in the kitchen where I dumped it before the Great After-School Snack Hunt and slide the small folder from it. Already tingling with nerves, I plant myself at the empty end of kitchen table, the folder clutched in my hand. Mum's at the other end, poring over her laptop, coffee at her side. My mother can drink coffee all day and night and then just go to sleep whenever she wants like she hasn't been sucking down stimulants all day. It defies all laws of physiology.

She shoots me a quick smile over the glow of her screen. "All good, hon?"

I nod, and she goes back to her work. I like that we can do that. I know Mum's super busy, and she knows I'm doing something or I wouldn't be here. I love the way she never gets in my face. But I know if I needed her for something, she'd stop what she was doing straight away.

I open the folder and take a breath, and when I'm completely ready, I lean over the sheet. The happiness is instant. Even in these miniature versions, I can see some of the pictures are as awesome as I hoped they would be. The shapes Stella made with her body are amazing, of course. The light is great too. I changed it around a lot. For some, I had the blinds wide open, trying to get as much natural morning light in. For others, I shut them and turned on the harsher fluorescent lights. For others, I used nothing, so she was reduced to being a shadow figure. In one picture, I've caught her midleap, with not a trace of blur. Miraculous, considering the low light. There are other less spectacular ones I love too. A close up of just her fingers stretched out to the light. One photo of a thick strand of her hair whirling around her taut neck as she turns. One of her profile as she looks up, mid-dance, by the open studio door, the morning sun grazing her cheekbones and making her eyes even paler.

I sit back in my seat and grin like an idiot. Here's the thing: there's nothing, *nothing*, better than the feeling you get when you discover you managed to capture exactly what you wanted to capture. Sure, some of these images might not turn out as good at full size, but for now, I'm happy.

I go to bed feeling pretty damn good. I pull my doona to my chest and rest my computer on my lap. That's when Stella finally replies.

> *Bad moment, I guess. I'd love to see the photos, if you'll still let me.*

I smile and type.

> *Of course I will.*

I cannot lie. I can't wait to show her.

CHAPTER 27

The next day in Drama class, we all muddle through warm-ups and improv. And it's not just me being half-hearted about it for once. Even Antony and the other more serious kids are lacklustre today. I can tell from the nervous energy in the room that it's because we're all just waiting for Peter to tell us which groups he's picked to be in the showcase.

Ashani's pretty confident we'll be one of them. She says only one other group was really good. They did this five-minute play about homelessness. I'm praying we'll win a spot. Not just because I love what we made but because I actually want to see it this time. I want to see what it looks like when my images and Ashani's words and Stella's choreography come together properly. I still get the guilts when I think about missing that.

We drag our feet through the forty minutes, making eye-rolling contact with each other every now and then and silently enduring. Finally, it's over and Peter claps his hands. This time, instead of the usual thirty seconds it takes everyone to settle down, silence descends instantly.

"Listen, people," he booms. "You all did a great job with the assignment, and you came up with some really original and engaging ideas. I can only put three of the performances into the showcase schedule, as you know, and the ones I have chosen were selected for three reasons. First, because they worked to the brief. They truly attempted to illustrate how theatre can have a social and political purpose. But I also selected them based on how well they were performed and how they will work on the auditorium stage. These are the three I have chosen."

The room is still. Stiller than I have ever seen a group of Year 10 kids in my life. Our group is named third. And the moment Peter says it, Michael lets out this holler and a whistle and all of our group cracks up. High fives all round. I take a deep breath and grin. I'm getting a second chance with this thing.

After class we decide to go to the café and dwell in our self-satisfaction with beverages. Grumpy Waitress dumps our drinks on our table, still surly even though we all actually order something for once.

"This is so awesome," Michael says, leaning back in his seat and smiling. "Now my parents can see it. And maybe they'll stop whinging about me doing dance on the weekends instead of maths homework."

"And now I've got a proper directorial piece under my belt," Ashani says. "Like, an actual stage performance."

"Is that what you want to do?" I ask her. "Be a director?" I didn't realise it was an actual career aspiration.

"Only all my life."

"You'll be great at it." She will. Because I know now that all the qualities about Ashani that are kind of annoying will probably make her brilliant at that job.

"Thanks," she says. "The course is ridiculously competitive, though. Most people who apply straight out of high school are told to go away and get more experience first."

"What do you want to do, Zel?" Stella asks. "I mean, at uni. Photography?"

I shake my head. My uncle's a commercial photographer, and all he does is take photos of food and kitchenware for catalogues and websites. I don't think I'd like that. I want to keep photography for fun. "Maybe psychology? I'm not sure yet."

Antony turns to Stella. "And you'll dance, I guess?"

She shakes her head. "I'm not good enough."

"What?" Me and Michael both say it at once.

I find that hard to believe. I don't know much about dancing, but she seems good enough to me.

"But you're amazing," Michael says.

"I'm not good enough for a company or anything." She shrugs. "I'll definitely go to a uni with a dance program, and I'd love to teach dance, but that's it."

"I'm going to do engineering like Dad," Michael says. "And Ant's applying for drama school, right?"

"Correct."

I grin at him. "What does Rosa say about that?"

"A lot, as you can imagine."

"Yeah, I can."

Stella and I walk home together, her hauling her bike and me lugging my backpack loaded down with books. I have *so* much homework to do. So does Stella, she says. So I don't know if it's because the sun's shining or because of the spectre of homework hanging over our heads, but we dawdle. We don't talk much, but I'm used to it now. I've spent more time in silence with this girl than I have talking to her. I'm also starting to get that Stella doesn't really talk unless she's got something to say. And now that I've seen her dance, I wonder if maybe it's because she does all her best communicating that way.

When we hit the park near the end of my street, she waves at the stretch of grass. "Want to hang out for a bit?"

I squint at her for a second. "Uh, sure."

She rests her bike against a rock and flops down on the grass, stretching out her legs in front of her. I remember the contact sheet in my bag as I sit down. I've been keeping it in there so I don't forget to take it back to photography class next week. I hesitate for a minute. Part of me wants to wait until I've developed the actual photos to show her, but the other part wants to show her right now. To show them off. Show what I can do. And what she can be.

Ego wins. I slide the sheet out and hold it in front of her without saying a word. She stares at it for a second and then takes it, holding it close to her face. "They're so tiny."

"It's a contact sheet. You use it to decide which images work before you develop them in large. Saves time and money."

She nods and leans against the rock, shielding her eyes and staring at the images. She looks for a lot longer than most people usually do. Finally she passes them back to me. "You're *really* good."

I slip the sheet back into my bag, out of the sun. "*You're* really good." I lie back on the grass. The clouds are all streaky wisps today, like they've been blown in from somewhere in a hurry. I wonder where they've come from.

Stella pulls her knees to her chest and twirls a grass blade between her fingers. "You know that girl the other day? When you saw me and Ollie?"

"Yeah. The one you don't seem to like very much." I squint up at her. "At least you didn't look like you do."

She tears the grass into tiny strips. "We were together for a while. Over summer."

Is it weird that I blush at that revelation? I feel like it is. And I don't respond straight away either, because I'm too busy trying to compute the fact that Stella dates girls. Or has at least has dated one. Nope. Definitely didn't see that one coming. Didn't even enter my mind as a vague possibility.

What kind of failed gay am I? Unable to spot my own kind. I mean, let's be honest. This is the kind of thing that comes up in my mind a lot. And usually in the hopeful way. I think it's safe to say that if I had my way, all girls would be lesbians. Then I wouldn't be constantly negotiating the terrifying landmine-strewn land of *is she or isn't she?* Mostly because I'm too scared to ever just ask. Meanwhile, this one goes completely undetected.

And even though I'm buzzing with this new information, I go the *no big deal* route. "So what happened?"

"I don't know."

I wait to see if she's going to say more. She doesn't. "Has anyone ever told you that you're really easy to talk to?"

She raises an eyebrow. "No."

"That's not surprising."

And she laughs. Actually laughs. And if I wasn't lying down already, I'd probably fall over.

"I'm sorry," she says, still smiling. "What can I tell you? The thing with Fia lasted about a minute, but it was long enough to hurt. A lot." The smiles slides away. "And even though I'm over her, I still feel kind of angry that I let someone treat me like crap."

"You *should* be angry about that."

"And I can't stand the way when she sees me, she stops and chats like we're old buddies or something, instead of remembering that she started it and then dumped me five minutes later."

"Break-ups are crappy enough without people pretending they aren't." And in the spirit of her actually sharing something, I feel like I want to tell her something in return. "I was with someone just before I came here." I don't really know why I'm avoiding gender pronouns here. It's not like she's going to be weird. "But after I moved, there was just this silence. Nothing. And then that day of the Drama performance, when I was sick?"

"You mean when you *weren't* sick."

I open my eyes. "You knew?"

"Well, I knew you were really into the project and that if you really were just sick, you probably still would have tried to come. I knew it had to be something else."

I blink, trying to take in the ways this girl seems to have gotten to know me without me even noticing. "Yeah, well, the something else was me finally hearing from them." I correct myself. "From her." I wait a beat for a reaction, but there's none. "And even though I knew she was probably not going to tell me anything I wanted to hear, it was still awful to actually hear the words said. And there was other stuff too. Her stuff. Stuff that made me feel even worse about it all."

And before I know it, I'm telling her about Prim. I give her the short version of how we made friends, the subway project, and my crush. I tell her about Coney Island and the kiss and how she never came to meet me on that last trip. I don't tell her the rest. Prim's stuff. I still don't think I'm brave enough yet to face the ways in which someone I worshipped might have even more than just the regular, human kind of fragile. It's easier to feel miserable than responsible for someone else's misery, I guess.

When I'm done talking, she's quiet for a minute. "I'm sorry," she finally says. "That must have been hard."

"It was." I sit up and rest my chin on my knees. Stella plucks some grass from the back of my jumper. I smile at her. "Thanks. See, here's the thing—"

"You always say that."

"What?"

"'Here's the thing.'" She grins at me. "You start with it a lot."

"I do?"

"Yup."

"Oh." I've never noticed. "Well, what I was going to say, before I was rudely interrupted…"

She rolls her eyes, but she's smiling. "Go on."

"This love crap is hard, isn't it?"

"Well, Fia's my only experience of any of it, really. So I'm going to go with yes."

"Same with me and Prim."

We both flop back onto the grass at the same time. I smile but say nothing. We lie there for a while, not talking. Instead, I watch Stella tie knots in a long piece of grass and enjoy the sun on my face. It's nice just being here with someone who knows a little bit what it feels like to be me. I want to ask her other stuff, like when she knew she was gay and how she knew and all those things, but they'll keep. Right now, there's as much comfort in this silence, in just being here with her, so I go with it.

And miracle of miracles, not one single member of Stella's family rings or messages in the time we're lying there. And when the sun drops low and the wind picks up and we're finally forced to think about abandoning our patch of grass, I say, "I think that's the first time I've ever hung out with you without you having to suddenly run off."

"Just call me Cinderella."

I stand up and hold out my hand. She puts her slim, pale one in mine, and I haul her up. When we're face-to-face again, she stares at me for a moment, chewing her lip. "Can I ask you something? Something else?"

"Uh, sure?"

"I was wondering, when you've developed those photos, if I could maybe buy some?" Before I can respond, she hurries on. "It's just that the only dance photos I've got are dumb old ones of me posing in tutus, grinning like an idiot from my baby ballet days. And I feel like if I ever looked back, the ones you took are how I'll remember dance."

She crosses her arms across her chest and smiles. She always does that, I realise, crosses her arms when she's talking about herself. Like she thinks she shouldn't be. She bites her lip. "You're so good, and I love your pictures. They're raw. They actually look like dance feels, you know?"

And I smile at her, because it's the biggest compliment I've ever received in my life. "Stell, you idiot. I'll *give* you the photos."

Chapter 28

Antony and I sit on a log at the edge of the garden, watching some of our cousins play on the grass. Behind us in the restaurant, the relatives are drinking after-lunch coffees and chatting. They could go on all afternoon.

He's telling me about a drama program he's auditioning for next week. It's this intensive weekend thing, attached to a big theatre. Only a few kids get into it each term.

"I have to memorise *two* monologues," he tells me, pulling a face.

"You want help?" I swat a bug away. "I can read with you, if you want."

"Really, you'd help?"

"Of course." I nudge his shoulder. Why does he think I wouldn't? He's my cousin. And my friend.

"That'd be great. Ashani offered to help me out, but last time she did that with the school play last year, she kept interrupting and giving me all these instructions."

"Of course she did." We give each other these eye-rolling grins.

"She's awesome," he says hurriedly. "But I *know* how to act."

I nod, because he really does. Antony is easily the best in our class. "I'll help, and I promise I won't offer any advice." Ha, imagine me giving acting advice.

I watch Madi boss Simone through some game on the grass. I nudge him. "Sometimes it's so strange that you want to act. Remember when we were their age?" I point at the girls. "How shy you were? It was hard enough to get you to speak."

He nods. "Mum thought there had to be something wrong with me just because I wasn't a bigmouth like everyone else in the family." He snaps a twig off a branch and starts to break it into little pieces. "I think I only started to feel like I was weird because Mum made such a big deal about it." He sighs. "I don't know why I was like that. I just didn't like to talk, and I didn't really like other kids that much then."

"You liked me," I remind him. At least I think he did.

"Because you were the only one who treated me like I was normal. Or at least like being different was fine. I always liked it when I got to see you in Canberra. You didn't care if I was shy or that I was difficult to get to know. You were always so chill and funny."

"I just wanted to play with you. So I kept trying." I recall what Dad told me the other day, about me and difficult people. Maybe he's right. Maybe that's how I've ended up with my Prims and my Antonys. And maybe my Stellas too. I don't write them off straight away as difficult, even if they're hard work.

The sun emerges briefly from behind a cloud, and Antony tips his face towards it. I notice whiskers pushing out of his chin. "When I got to high school," he says, "I think being weird and eccentric became my defence. Or my revenge on Mum and Dad, I don't know. But I'm glad I did, because I got to change schools. That's how I found theatre. And my own bunch of weirdos." He smiles.

"*Our* bunch of weirdos now. Thanks for sharing."

"You're most welcome," he says, bowing his head, all chivalrous.

"Hang on, does that mean I'm a weirdo?"

"Nah. But I think you have a thing for them."

It's true. I do. Including this cousin of mine. I bump my shoulder against his again. And because we've known each other all our lives, I know he understands what I'm trying to tell him.

We go back to watching the kids for a while. Then I remember what I've been wanting to ask him for ages.

"Hey?"

"What?"

"Are you ever going to just ask Ashani out?"

His face turns redder than his shirt. "I don't know."

"You better get in before Michael does."

"I know," is all he says.

~ ~ ~

So, if I never wrote Antony off as too hard, part of me knows I shouldn't write Prim off now either. That's why I finally bring myself to pull the Coney Island photos out from where they have been sitting on my camera and develop the negatives. While in some ways I'd be happy to resign that trip to the memory graveyard forever, I also know there are some great pictures from the boardwalk and Brighton Beach in there, and I need them for my project. Art, in this case, is going to have to trump heartbreak. But I also know that there's a little music-facing in the Prim department to be done.

I didn't know I'd actually be facing *her*, though. Well, the image of her. I'm sitting in the darkroom at school, sorting through the negatives, when I see it: a picture of Prim. I should probably tell you that I never really took photos of Prim. For so many reasons. One, because I felt self-conscious paying that close attention to her. Two, because she hated it (awesome for a future model, right?). Three, because I was usually too caught up in taking photos of the places we were in.

Somehow, even though I feel like every moment of that day on Coney Island is etched into my memory bank, I don't remember taking this shot. It was supposed to be goofy: Prim in a shop, wearing one of those furry Russian hats we'd seen the oldies on the pier wearing. But because it's Prim and it turns out she's even more radiant on camera than in person, it's actually beautiful. She's staring down the camera, her mouth pursed into a scowl with eyes six feet wide and this haughty lift in her chin. And she makes it look good.

I stare at the photo, still that stunned I forgot taking it. But as I sit there with it clasped in my hand, I realise that the sight of Prim doesn't do what it used to. It doesn't give me that squeaky feeling I used to get back before Coney Island. What I feel now is sorrow, and sadness, and a little bit of…. Well, I don't want to say pity. Prim would hate it if I felt pity for her. But that's what it is. I feel pity that she has to feel or *not feel* what she does and that it makes her feel like a stranger in the world. And that she's never told someone until now.

What it also does is make me miss her. Prim is odd and cranky and a loose cannon, but she's *my* odd, cranky loose cannon of a best friend. I know that for certain. And she needs me.

I think about what she told me on Skype. All the things she surrendered to me and maybe all the things she'd surrendered before. Things like letting me see her home and telling me about her dad. I realise now that I made the error of mistaking the things that made Prim suffer—her ability to epically not give a crap, her ability to completely disregard people and march through life with her elbows out— for things that made her superhuman. And all that time, she was thinking that those things somehow made her less human.

I guess I've learned the hard way that she's just a girl. A girl with hardly any friends and an attitude that's probably going to keep her more alone than not in life. But she's also special and strange and combatively sweet. And if she lets you in, you feel special too. That's part of why things got so messed up, I guess. I thought that specialness meant something more.

I peg the negative to a piece of string and ask myself some vital questions:

Can I imagine her not being in my life?

And just asking myself that makes my heart do this achy squeezing thing. No, I can't imagine it.

Do I care that she doesn't want to be with me?

I wait for that heart squeeze, but it doesn't come this time. And you know what? Maybe I'm not that surprised. I think I've known for a long time, way before she told me. Probably before I even left New York. Here's the thing: even when you're sixteen and lovestruck and dumb, you have to know that hers was not the reaction of someone who really liked another person. And it feels even better to know that this is okay, that I can live with that. And when it comes down to it, I think most of my heartbreak has really just been about losing her as a person. About losing my best friend.

I guess I'm starting to realise that when you're gay, this stuff can get kind of messy. The lines between friendships and romance and feelings with girls are harder to draw. Maybe it's not just when you're gay. Maybe it's just being a teenager. I don't know.

But for now, here's what I know: I have to find a way for Prim to be in my life again, on the right terms and in the right way. Because I miss her like hell.

~ ~ ~

Life gets busy. It's the last two weeks of term, and everything's piling up the way it does. In fact, we might need another training montage here to cover the fiesta of high achievement my life has become.

For one, I've got homework coming out my ear and I'm getting it done. There's a Psych assignment, a talk for English, and the reflection on our part of the Drama project to do. (Of course they don't just let you *do* drama at our school. We have to write about it to get the marks.) Every night, I'm trying to power through it all.

We also have a couple of rehearsals scheduled for the showcase, because Peter wants us to get used to the stage. At rehearsals I don't have much to do, just sit with Ashani and watch the others. So I do. But really, I watch Stella, because how can I not? She's incredible. Even now I've seen her dancing a lot now, I just can't reconcile the reserved, sometimes surly (but maybe secretly sweet) Stella with this creature I see onstage.

The subway project is going pretty well. I should stop calling it that, really, because it's got nothing to do with the subway project anymore now that I've come up with this movement angle. I have this idea to mount the pictures on maps. It might be lame, but Stedman's okay with it, and I think I've firmly established that Stedman's go-ahead is some kind of holy grail of Year 10 art class, so I'm going with it.

Then, to top it all off, my new photography teacher decides we should put on a little show at the end of our term. She's going to select a series of our images to show, and we're supposed to invite our parents and friends to come see them. My class pals, Miriam and Wayne, are in a tizzy about it. Wayne's got right into nature photography, and he's developed a zillion photos. They're mostly close-ups of flowers, though. Real snooze stuff for me, but he loves them. Miriam has been doing portraits. Some of them are really good, but she's terrified none of them will get picked. I'm hoping the photos of Stella will make the grade when I develop them.

So much is happening. I've barely seen Mum and Dad, and I definitely haven't had a minute to decide how or when to make contact with Prim. I get pangs of guilt every now and then that she bared her feelings and I've given her nothing in return.

I will. I just need a minute to figure out how to make it right.

CHAPTER 29

The photos are perfect. I think they might be some of the best photos I've ever taken. And because I can't wait for her to see them, I message Stella to see what she's doing. But still, I'm surprised when she immediately invites me to come by her place.

Her house is way bigger than mine. Not in the posh sense, just in the needing to fit more people way. I knock on the door. And even though I can hear a lot of noise inside, no one answers straight away. When someone finally does appear, it's her.

"Hey." She's in her dance leggings, but her hair is out, the long red strands falling around her shoulders. She should always wear it like that.

"I've got the photos," I say instead of hello.

She steps aside, letting me in. There are people everywhere. There are three guys in the lounge room, chatting loudly about sport. Brothers, I guess. I can hear clanking noises, from what I guess is the kitchen, and the sound of someone talking loudly on the phone. Ollie is kneeling on the stairs, running a stick back and forth between the wooden railings, just like he did with the fence that day I met him. "The latest obsession," Stella says as we watch him.

I fight the urge to clap my hands over my ears. No wonder Stella's so quiet all the time. This place makes me realise how peaceful my only-child house is. A definite perk.

Stella climbs the first few steps, leans down and kisses Ollie's head, and then beckons to me. "It's quieter upstairs. Relatively."

I grin and follow her past her brother to a room near the back of the house. It's a biggish room, but it's cramped. There's two of everything: beds, desks, wardrobes, chairs.

"My sister and I share, but she's nearly always at her boyfriend's." Stella leans on the windowsill and watches me look around.

It's easy to tell two very different people live in here. Even though the furniture kind of matches, the colours, the posters, and the bedspreads are all different.

She folds her arms. "Can you tell which side's mine?"

I smirk and point at one side.

"How did you know?"

"Um…" I point at the postcard of a dancer doing a balance on a railing, backlit by the sun. "Kind of obvious."

Her face falls. "Oh. Yeah."

"Well, I have more pictures for your collection." I take out the envelope and give it to her.

She looks through the pictures slowly, saying nothing. Then she tucks them back in the envelope and gives me this shy smile. "Thank you."

"You're welcome." I watch her put them in her drawer. "Not going to hang them on your wall?"

She shakes her head. "Nope. They're just for me. To remember."

I nod, although I don't completely understand. If I could do what she does, I'd totally show it off.

She pushes herself away from the windowsill. "I know I've said this before, but you're a really good photographer."

"Thanks."

Then she just stands there, rubbing her arm absently, looking at me like she doesn't know what to do now. And because she still doesn't say anything, I wonder if she's waiting for me to leave. I go to say I should probably get home, and that's when she finally speaks. "So, what are you doing now? Do you want a tea or something?"

"Uh, um, I don't know." Uh-oh. Her awkwardness is making me awkward.

"I mean, I could make some, if you, you know, want some." She bites down on her lip. It's cute the way she cringes at her own word vomit.

I grin at her. "And competing this week on Who Can Be Most Weird About a Beverage…"

That makes her laugh. "Okay." She holds up a hand, takes in a breath, and sets her shoulders—a picture of Stella determination. "I'm making tea. We're drinking it."

"Okay." It seems wisest to agree.

But instead of making tea, she's still standing there, smiling at me.

"Um, we're going to need tea for that," I remind her.

"I know." She swipes at my arm as she passes. "I was just trying to figure out if we should go downstairs or outside or something. But let's stay here. It's safer."

"Safer?" I raise an eyebrow. "Am I missing some important information about your family? Tell me, should I have prepared an escape plan?"

She yanks open the door and grins. "No, I just mean we'll be left alone. Instead of being roped into cooking or settling an argument. Or Ollie-sitting, of course. This is one of the few days I've had off the roster in a while. And while I love him, I'd like to keep it that way. I'll bring the tea here."

When she brings the tea up, we lie sideways on her bed and drink it. It's nearly dark outside now. She switches on her bedside lamp, and the room is cast in a dull, orange glow.

She turns to me. "You know that girl you told me about?"

"Yeah."

"Are you still upset about it?"

"Kind of." I try to tell her about what's been going through my head. "But I'm not sad because she doesn't want to be with me. I'm sad because she's not in my life anymore. She's so…" And as usual, I just can't explain or describe Prim. She defies explanation. I give her the bare bones version of what Prim said on Skype. "I wish I hadn't made her feel like that."

Stella tucks her arms under her head and settles back against a pillow. "But you didn't do it on purpose. You were just feeling your feelings. And she was feeling hers. I mean, if she kissed you back, you couldn't know it was for any other reason than she liked you too."

"I know. I just wish none of it happened."

"But it kind of had to, didn't it? So you could figure this stuff out?"

"I guess." I chew on that thought for a minute and then let out a slow breath. "I miss her. She's my best friend."

"Can you be friends again?"

"I hope so."

Stella rolls over onto her side, facing me. "I've been thinking about this stuff a lot. About what goes wrong between people. Like, with me and Fia, and even with my mum and dad. I think sometimes people meet because they connect and they're, you know, meant to be together, and it's all great. But sometimes people end up together just because their needs happen to collide at a point in time. It's more of a selfish thing."

"What do you mean?"

"Like with Fia and I. We weren't together because we connected especially. I think our needs met. Fia needed to feel someone's admiration. I needed to sort my gay stuff out, to test the waters. But that's not enough, is it?"

"No, it's not." I nod slowly, turning this idea over in my mind. "Sometimes I wonder if I just wanted Prim because I'd never had a girl really like me. And because I was kind of lonely in New York until I met her. I think we were probably just supposed to be friends."

"It's hard to know this stuff with girls and friendships sometimes, isn't it?"

I nod. It's good to know I'm not the only one who feels like that. "Tell me about it. You're talking to the girl who nearly wrecked a friendship by not knowing the difference."

She smiles and plays with the handle of her tea mug. I contemplate what she's said. And I contemplate *her*, this wise, weird girl with her odd little combination of physically elegant and socially clumsy.

"So," she says slowly. And it sounds like a question.

"What?"

"Do you think *we* connect?"

I stare at her. I wasn't expecting that. There's this weird feeling in my stomach, like I'm about to jump off something high. I nod, suddenly feeling crazy shy. "I think so. Do *you* think we do?"

She lifts her eyes from her cup for a fleeting second. "Yes."

"Why?"

"Because we surprise each other."

I nod. Maybe she's right, but I'm too busy fighting this weird, buzzy feeling. Something has changed, and I don't know how I feel about it or what to do about it. But all I know is that maybe I need a minute. Mostly because I don't want to crash through anything, to make a clumsy mess in that way I always seem to.

I sit up slowly and make a show of checking the time. "Hey, listen, I better go. Ton of homework."

She nods, but I can tell she's disappointed.

"We'll all hang out after the show on Friday, though, right?"

She nods again, staring down at the bed, drawing a little pattern with her finger. "Probably."

"Definitely," I tell her, feeling like I'm trying to make something better. "No babysitting plans, okay?"

She gives me a small smile. "No babysitting."

When she closes the front door behind me, I take in a great gulp of air and stride away, trying to put as much distance between me and the awkwardness I just created back there. But of course, it follows me.

I walk down the street, my brain refusing to move on from this shiny, new, ineluctable little fact I now possess. *She likes me.* Stella likes me. I know it in my gut. I shake my head as I walk. It's so strange. I've never *known* something like that before. I've always wanted to, but usually I'm stuck in that state of wondering or hoping. It's never just the stunning, unnerving simplicity of knowing. But now it's here, in full stereo, and all I can do is blink and walk away. And I have no idea if it's the dumbest or the smartest thing I have ever done.

~ ~ ~

When I wake up in the morning, the first thing I think about is last night and Stella. I wonder if she is upset at me for leaving. Or maybe she does just think I really had to go. I hope so. I don't want to hurt her feelings. I don't even know if I wanted to leave her in that moment. I just need to think.

So I go to the adult learning centre and shell out some of my pocket money to use the darkroom for a couple of hours, my form of meditation. I work on developing a bunch of photos from the subway project. Photos that I won't use in my art project, but ones I'd like to keep. To remember.

I'm looking at this picture of this old guy walking through Queens somewhere with a parrot on his shoulder. I remember how much Prim loved that guy. "When I get old, I want to be that weird," she told me.

"Don't worry, you will be," I replied and snapped the photo just as the bright bird nibbled at his ear and he smiled.

That's when I get the idea. I start going through all the contact sheets and negatives and finding all the Prim things. Things she noticed or commented on, or that I know she will remember. I gather them together, editing and sorting, working out which pictures to develop, curating our friendship into a story. Things like the funny grave in Woodlawn, the crazy old lady in the subway car who asked Prim if she was my mother, the public sign in the station that made it look like you could only ride the escalator if you had a dog with you. We are in none of the photos, yet we are always there. This, I decide, will be my gift to her.

I develop as many as I can, and then I move on to the photos I'm using in my end-of-term show for my photography class. I pull out the three photos I have chosen. They're all of Stella, from that day at the studio. I haven't told her yet, but I'm going to use them. They're too good not to. She's too good not to.

CHAPTER 30

Mum and Dad are at the Parent Showcase. So are Rosa and Madi. All our parents are there, actually. Even Michael's. Even though they tell him to quit dancing all the time and to focus on his studies.

This time Ashani asks me to start the sound and visuals. She wants to watch it from the front. I never thought I'd see her relinquish control, even the simple push of a button, but she does. And of course I say yes. I need to make up for last time. I stand there at the panel while Peter introduces the three acts. We're the first of the Drama groups.

Peter's got his best drama voice on. And even from here, I can tell the parents are hanging onto every word. "I asked the Year 10 students to explore the notion of home and to create a piece of theatre with a social purpose. And the three performances you are about to see are from groups that exceeded my expectations. They—"

Suddenly I'm not hearing anything, because Stella's standing next to me. She bounces up and down a little on her toes and smiles at me. And that smile floods me with relief. She's not mad.

"Nervous?"

She shakes her head. "Excited." And I believe her. She looks positively serene. That's what dance does to her.

I look at Michael and Antony a few feet away, stretching. They look more like I'd look if I were about to go onstage in front of all those people—terrified.

There's a round of applause, and Peter strides backstage, giving us a thumbs-up. I feel a quick squeeze of my fingers before Stella moves forward, stepping out onstage. Beside me, someone cues the lights. And when I see their shadowy shapes posed, ready to begin, I hit play.

The whole performance, I know I should be worrying about if it's going completely right, if the boys are hitting their steps, if people are liking it, but I can only stare at her. I can only zero in on that fluid way she moves, the way she possesses her entire body and kind of speaks with it. I can't believe she doesn't think she's good enough to be a real professional dancer. I think she's wrong, and I'm going to tell her that a thousand times over until she hears me.

While I'm standing there, watching, and the voices play over their steps, I hear a line I've heard a thousand times now as Ashani and I worked to get the sound and visuals to work together perfectly. "I think home is people, really, more than place." Maybe that's true.

After the performance, Michael and Stella and I take jars to the door of the auditorium and hold them out to the parents above a giant poster I've made. Last week I contacted the Asylum Seeker Centre and asked if I could raise money for them. I'm glad I did, because the parents are loving it. They coo over our performance and make a big show of opening wallets and purses to donate. Some of them even hand over not just coins but notes. Even some of the students give money. It makes me think that maybe we can find more ways of helping. For now, this feels pretty good, though. And Dad knows it, because when he and Mum drop money in my jar, along with a big smacking kiss on my cheek, he says, "You found a way, kiddo."

I did.

Afterwards, we go out, the five of us, and eat pizza and laugh and talk up our drama abilities. And we promise we'll work on our next project together.

Stella elbows me. "You'll have to go onstage this time, you know."

"Yeah." Antony grins.

"And I will deal with that when we get there," I say loftily as I nudge Stella back.

"Don't worry, Z." Ashani stuffs a piece of pineapple in her mouth. "I'll write a killer part for a tree into it for you."

They laugh, but I think it's a genius plan.

Stella and I walk home together. We talk about the show some more. Safe territory, I guess.

"I'm so happy it was good," I say. "Not that I thought it wouldn't be," I hurry to add. "You guys were amazing, of course."

"You made it even better, you know, by raising money. That was really cool."

I shrug, playing nonchalant, but inside I'm golden. "I just wanted to help more."

She nods. "Yeah, and that's really cool. Maybe we can figure out other ways to help too. Maybe fundraising or volunteering or something. On the holidays."

I nod. "We should."

At the point where our paths diverge, she turns to me and smiles. I smile back, suddenly unable to think of a single thing to say. Neither, clearly, can she. And it feels so weird and loaded, especially because we've only just found the space where we can talk with ease. And now it's gone again.

"I better go," I finally say.

She bites her bottom lip and nods.

"I'll see you soon? We'll all hang out, right?"

"Of course," she says in this quiet voice.

We give each other these small smiles, and I turn away, even though my stomach's doing this fluttering thing that tells me I should probably stay. As soon as I hear her cycle off, I let out a loud sigh and swear instead of hitting myself, which is what I really want to do. Why am I walking away from her when I don't think I actually want to be?

~ ~ ~

The next day, I go back to the darkroom after school and finish the album for Prim. I keep it simple. No frills, no bows (as if) for Prim. Just a really nice, clean, black sketchbook with a photograph mounted on each crisp, white page. Underneath I write the subway line in neat black pen.

I take it home, wrap it carefully, and place it on my desk. Now I just have to think of the right words to send with it. Whether Prim likes it or not, this one's going to need at least a few words. But just having the book there ready to go gives me this sense of relief. I have found the way to tell her how much she means to me in a way she'll understand. Because there's no one but me and her who will see the value in the contents of this book. Sure, they might see some passably decent photographs, but they won't have a clue what it took to get them.

I wander into the kitchen. Mum's there, standing at the bench, staring at her phone and eating toast. She smiles when she sees me. "First night of your holidays, Zel. What are you doing here?"

I shrug. "I don't know." At least compared to a month ago, I have options. I could be hanging out with Antony and the others. Or Stella.

Stella.

I think of the look on her face last night. She was smiling but kind of pensive, like she was worried too. And I know I put that look there. And suddenly, picturing that face while I stand on the cold lino in my bare feet, I know I want to make it go away. I turn for my room. "Actually, you're right. I'm going out."

"Uh, okay, bye," I hear her mutter as I dash to my room to find shoes.

When I get to her house, the front door opens before I can knock. An older girl with the same red hair as Stella carries a huge, white handbag and wears a face full of make-up. At the sight of me standing there, probably looking as tremulous as I feel, she blinks and gives me a brief, questioning smile.

"Hey, is Stella home?"

Is it just me, or does she raise her eyebrow a fraction? Then she nods and turns and opens her mouth as if she's about to call out to her.

I hold up a hand. "It's cool. Is she in her room? I can just go up."

The girl turns to me with this knowing smile. "Sure, have fun." She slides out past me and into the night, her heels clicking on the concrete.

I make my way slowly up the stairs, suddenly nervous now. The house is as noisy as last night, but I can't actually see anyone. I knock on her bedroom door.

"Yeah?" She sounds anything but happy about the intrusion.

Ignoring the shaky feeling in my legs, I push the door open. She's sitting cross-legged on her bed, looking at her phone. Her eyes widen when she sees me.

I smile nervously. "Your sister let me in. At least, I think it was your sister. Kind of fancy?"

Stella laughs. "If shovelled-on make-up is your idea of fancy, then that's my sister."

"So, can I come in?"

"Uh, sure." But at the same time, she scoots back against her pillow and does that thing where she folds her arms across her chest.

I shut the door behind me and sit tentatively on the edge of her mattress. She looks at me kind of warily. I guess I would too, though, if she'd just rocked up out of nowhere and planted herself on my bed. Especially after all this vague, unspoken weirdness has blown in from somewhere and solidified between us in the last forty-eight hours. But I'm too busy feeling all fluttery and nervous to know how to make *her* feel better. But I also want her to know that I want to be nowhere else but sitting on the edge of her bed, my stomach invaded by an army of disgruntled butterflies. Because it still feels *right*.

That's when you know it, isn't it? When a girl makes you feel nervous and excited but at home all at the same time?

And because I can't think of a single word to say, I just move closer. Her arms are still wrapped tightly around her, but I gather all my courage and clasp one of her wrists. I gently draw her arm towards me and take her hand. As my fingers slide over her palm, she bites down on her lip and stares at this new fact of us touching. Her smile is hesitant. I decide to consider that permission to approach and lean to drop a small kiss on her smiling mouth.

"What about when I surprise you like that?" I whisper, blushing as I hear her take in a sharp, little breath. "When I surprise *me* like that," I add. My face is still kind of close to hers, and my grin is playful. But my heart feels like it's slowing to a stop while I wait for her to react. The next thing I know, I'm back in that place where my fears live. Have I just made another reckless, dumb mistake with a girl? But before I can sit back, she reaches out and gently cups my neck with her hand, stopping me in my tracks. And it feels *incredible*. And I want to keep surprising her. Maybe forever.

Then she smiles like I've never really seen her do before, full and frank. "Yes. I like it. A lot." Her eyes narrow as she smiles, and it's the kind of look that makes me pull in a breath, even though I wasn't ready to. It's the kind of smile that makes me want to kiss her again. So I lean in and press my mouth to hers, and those fingers on the back of my neck grip a little tighter. I can both hear and feel the quickening of her breath, and I know it's okay. More than okay.

It's a longer kiss this time. Long enough for me to learn the shape of her mouth and for her hand to glide down my back and up again before threading into my hair. And as her hand explores, there's this shimmer radiating through me. Kissing never felt like this before. With Jonna, I only felt this kind of heated curiosity. With Prim, it was too brief and terrifying. This is different. This is the feeling of two people wanting the same thing at the same time. And it's awesome and lovely and electric all at the same time. I think this is what it's *supposed* to feel like.

Eventually we pull away, but not far away. And as I meet her eye, she gives me that look. You know that look where someone is silently asking a question? I know from the timidity of her stare that it's something like *are you just doing this or do you really want to do this*? And I don't possess the words yet to tell her what I've just discovered, that, yes, I really *really* want to do this. With her. So much. I nod, even though she didn't ask the question and hope she knows why. I kiss her again, just to make my point. Okay, I kiss because I really want to kiss her again.

I know, I know, shut up. I'm fully aware that this has possibly been one of those things, hasn't it? Where you guys have been sitting back, watching us give each other meaningful looks, just waiting for us to get together already? I know I would have.

And yes, the ship has finally sailed. But don't be smug. It's totally easy to stare, glued to the screen or flipping pages, thinking, "Oh, come on! When are they going to figure it out?" I do it all the time. But you should know it's also a *lot* harder to figure this stuff out in real life than it is in books and movies. And maybe I'm a dummy at this, but I figured it out in the end, okay?

So we lie on the bed, sometimes kissing, sometimes just being, as darkness falls completely. I run my fingers over her cheek, acquainting myself with the scatter of her freckles as she smooths her fingers through my hair. There's this sensation, like being submerged in water, where you can feel the hollowness of your chest, the push of the air on the walls of your lungs. I feel like that now. It's strange but good.

And luckily, even though it feels like people are constantly moving around this house, clattering up and down the stairs and stomping in and out of rooms, no one comes near us. This is something that Stella quietly assures me is nothing less than a miracle. Still, the threat's there, so even though we're all curled up on her bed alone, we keep it pretty G-rated. Besides, I think as I run my finger slowly over the sharp ridge of her collarbone, I get the feeling we're both into taking our time. Because we have it. Lots of it. There's no hurry. So we lie there, wrapped up in each other as doors slam, phones ring, and toilets flush around us. And as the bustle of the house eventually slows and that noisy, relentless cycle of coming and going ebbs, we just curl in closer around this space we've made together.

When we finally are disturbed, it's her little brother. But he does nothing more than open the door and stand there, staring mutely for a minute before he makes an abrupt turn and leaves.

"That was kind of creepy," I can't help saying.

"Trust me, you get used to it. He always knows what's going on in the house. It's like some part of his brain is always keeping tabs, even if he's totally busy doing all the stuff he does. Somewhere in there, he'll remember that a virtual stranger went upstairs and still hasn't left. Clearly, he decided it was time to check up on us."

"If you've got a Saturday night off from Ollie-sitting, what are you doing home?" I ask her, lacing my fingers through hers and holding our hands up in the air where I can stare at the newness of them entwined.

"No plans." She pulls my hand down and kisses the back of it. "I'm not exactly rolling in posse, you know. There's you guys, and then there's my dance friends. But we usually only hang out after class. And I can only watch the boys drool over Ashani so much. So I stay home a lot."

"I get it. A shocking amount of my social life revolves around my parents and my living room."

"It's better than having it revolve around a seven-year-old."

"True." I press my face into her hair, breathing in deep. I can smell that pretty watermelon-but-not scent from the day of the dress rehearsal. I squeeze her hand, remembering the feeling of dancing with her that night, spinning around the garden, laughing. I wonder why I didn't figure it out then. "So, what would you do if you could tonight?"

I can feel her shrug. "I don't know. Just be out in the world."

"Let's do it."

"What? Go out?"

"Yes, go out." I sit up. I have this compelling urge to *be* with her, to exist in the world with her. Maybe it's a way of consolidating it, to make us a real thing. "Let's go out and walk around. Maybe eat or see a movie. Act like real human teenage people."

"I think if we were real human teenage people, we'd probably be out seeing some significant band or glued to Tinder or shagging in alleyways."

"We can do that if you want."

She laughs. "No, I'm happy with the senior citizen options. Probably better for my form at dance tomorrow."

"Good." I grab her by her wrists and pull her so she's sitting up next to me. "Let's go out, then."

But instead of getting up, she just sits there, biting her lip.

I wonder why she's hesitating, and then it hits me. I hold up my hands. "Oh, hey, we can just go and hang out together. We don't have to be…gay about it if you're not into that. It's totally fine." The words pour out in a clumsy rush.

I'm not surprised when she laughs. I sound like an idiot. Why am I such an embarrassing bumbler? I grin and shrug and hope it's at least a little charming. "You know what I mean. We can be chill. Play platonic."

She smiles and puts her hand on my knee. It gives me a little shiver. How many brand new feelings can someone feel in one day? I watch her slender fingers play with a faded patch on the knee of my jeans. I've never seen someone with such elegant hands before.

"It's not that, exactly."

"Then what?"

Finally, after what feels like an eternity, she lifts her head and meets my eye. "I've liked you for a while, you know."

"You have?" I think of all the silences, the brush-offs, the general air of disinterest. *Really?* I pull a face at her. "I've got to say, you have a really terrible way of showing it."

She presses a hand to her face and cringes. "I'm sorry. I know. My brand of awkward can easily read as asshole. It's so dumb. I get shy, and then I get silent. But I've liked you ever since that day you first told off Ashani. Not because you told off Ashani, exactly, but just because you seemed so feisty and smart. Not to mention cute." She looks embarrassed now. *That* is cute. I pull her hand away from her face and give her the huge, dumb, enchanted smile I know is pasted to my face right now.

She pulls in another breath and continues. "But I feel like this—whatever this is—just kind of happened for you, and I don't know. I can't do another Fia." She shakes her head. "I don't…"

"Hey." I squeeze her hand. "This is not another Fia. I *promise*."

She's right, though. I guess it kind of did just happen. But that was only the realising part. When I look back on that night in the garden or that morning at the dance studio, when I think about my relentless curiosity about her, even when she could be so stand-offish, I see how maybe those feelings were already there a little.

But you know what? It's also one of those things in life that when it happens, it suddenly makes such perfect, total, amazing sense. So much so, you wonder how the hell you didn't think of it earlier. This is so different from what it was like with Prim. And that's because I can *feel* Stella feeling it too.

In fact, now even her weirdness makes sense, that edge of tension I could sense but couldn't read when I got to the house the other night. And because I need her to know, to feel as trusting and as certain as I do, I muddle my way through telling her all this. Her slow, sweet smile tells me she gets it.

"You kind of had an unfair advantage," I add.

She scrunches her face. "How's that?"

"Antony told you I was gay, didn't he?"

"Maybe." She grins. "Okay, yeah. He told us before you even came to the school how your whole family seemed to be discussing whether or not he might be gay, while there, quietly in the background the whole time, was you just doing your gay thing."

I laugh. Poor Antony. "See? You knew about me. I only just found out you were into girls two weeks ago, remember? It wasn't like I was aware it was even a possibility."

"Oh," she scoffs, climbing off the bed. "So it's my fault you have terrible gaydar?"

I laugh as she goes over to her dresser. She slips on a jumper and begins to run a brush through her hair. I guess we're going out into the world after all. Unable to stay away, I step over and wrap my arms around her waist. I pull her against me, feeling her narrow form against mine. "Stella?"

She turns around to face me. "What?"

My smile feels ten feet wide. "You're beautiful."

And I see something in her eyes let go at that moment. "I know," she says blithely and kisses me.

~ ~ ~

It's amazing and also completely dumb, isn't it, how when you start to like someone, they suddenly turn from being just someone you know into the most attractive thing in the world? You could have seen them every day for the last year and not noticed, and then suddenly, bam! They turn into something you can't take your eyes off. I mean, it's not like I didn't think Stella was pretty. I just didn't think about it that much. I was too full of Prim. But now I just want to stare at Stella, to map every constellation of freckles, to put a name to the precise shade of her skin, to note every changing shade of her hair in sunlight.

More than that, I want to touch her. When we're with the others, we play it cool, keeping our little secret for now. But when I'm around her, as we sit side by side, I'm constantly consumed by the need for something simple, like a press of our shoulders. I'll even settle for a touch of her foot to mine. So when she stealth-holds my hand under the table at a café for the first time, I feel like rays of light are shooting through me.

She talks now too. Talks with a need and an abandon that tells me that maybe she's just been waiting for our relationship to be what it should be before she could let go. She smiles more too. At me. And when she does, I get that feeling that Prim gave me when she touched my hair that day on City Island, only the sensation is slower and thicker but just as incredible. There are other things too, things she does especially for me: She waits for me by my locker before lunch so we can walk to the grass together and have a few minutes alone before we meet the others. And she wears her hair down more because I keep telling her it's beautiful. Now I can smooth my fingers through it when we lie in the park and stare at the sky or at each other.

I know things about her too. All kinds of things. There are so many things that it's hard to remember she was ever that mystifying silent girl. I know she can play the piano a little. I know her brothers called her Slinky because when she was little she was so skinny she could fit through the railings of their fence. I know her bike has a name: Mosey. I know she hates mushrooms but loves apricot jam on toast and has never seen my three favourite movies. I know that she's an evil tickler and an amazing kisser. And even though I already know all that, I want to know more. Because all these things feel like keys to a kingdom.

Okay, I'll shut up now.

CHAPTER 31

I wake up on the first Sunday of the school holidays and tell myself it's time. Now that I have a moment to breathe, I need to face the problem of Prim. I can't leave her soul-baring unanswered any longer. It's unfair and petty, even, to let my wounded (and not really wounded anymore) feelings make her feel worse about herself.

The sun shoots a shaft of light on my bed while I think about what Stella said that day in her room about liking people for the wrong reasons. And more and more, I think maybe she's right. Prim and I were never meant to be together. Our needs just happened to collide. Prim needed to feel close to someone. She's sharp and prickly, but she still needs to feel loved. I needed love too, but in a different way. And I was looking for it in the wrong person.

As I lie there, I cry a little, one last time for a friendship that nearly died. And for a friend who is so lost she can't find actual words to speak her heart. No one should feel like that. Now that I've committed to it, part of me wants to call or Skype, to get to her as soon as possible. But I know the very act of talking will just make it harder for her. And she would only read my grief for her as pity and hate me for it. So for her, I will hide all evidence of it behind words on a page.

Wiping my face, I climb out of bed, slide into the kitchen in my socks, and take an envelope and stamps from Mum's stash. I dash back to bed, and I don't get back out until I've found the words to fill the page. And you know what? It feels like the most grown-up thing I've ever done.

> Dear Prim,
> First, I'm sorry. I'm sorry for everything that went wrong between us. And I'm sorry that I made you feel bad. You are amazing, and you are enough for me in any way I get to have you in my life.

Now, before I shut up about it, because I know
you hate to talk about this stuff, I need you to
know this: You're my best friend and you always
will be. Also know that I love you and I miss you.
Dad says when he's finished this contract, he's
promised he'd go back to the company in NY for
a month. If it falls over school holidays, he says
he'll take me. So you better be there too. Not in
Milan or Paris, living that glamorous model life. And
then we'll go to Rockaway and see the Atlantic
like we're supposed to.
Until then, don't get famous and turn into an asshole.
This book is for you so you don't forget that we
are legends.
I love you, stupid.
Zel

I seal the envelope and place it in the parcel with the book. Then I dress and take it straight to the post box at the end of the street. Pushing it through the chute, I consign it to the whims of snail mail and the friendship gods. Then I turn for home.

As I leap up the path to my house, my phone buzzes. I smile at the sight of Stella's name. Because yes, I have turned into that disgustingly smitten sort of person who smiles like an idiot when their girlfriend messages. Yup, I've got it so bad you'll be glad I'm leaving you soon. Because you do *not* want to know how much I'm prepared to rave about this girl.

Want to come to the indoor pools? I'm taking Ollie.

I shamelessly decide to be the gross human being I have recently discovered I am capable of being. *You in not many clothes? I'm there.*

Well, there will also probably be a seven-year-old human limpet dangling from my neck the whole time. Not exactly sexy.

179

I grin.

Oh well. What time?

I change, grab my things, and head back out into that Sydney winter sunshine.

What she doesn't know either is what we're doing on the "date" I promised her tonight. I'm taking her to the community centre for the end-of-term photography show. And I'm going to show her a blown-up picture of herself, in full stereo dance mode, holding its own on the wall. Where she and her dancing should always be.

CHAPTER 32

"See what I mean?" Prim flips her hair over her shoulder and glares at the computer. At me. Then she does one of those walks where you inch along, placing one foot right in front of the other. And she counts as she walks. "Six, Zel! Six! It's TINY. My roommate is six feet away from me. Not even feet and inches feet. Human feet." She raises a hand. "*And* she eats peanut butter all the time. It stinks."

And because I know her so well, I ask. "What do you do to *her*, Prim?"

Prim grins and plants herself down in front of the computer again. "Not going to lie, I may have developed a penchant for natto lately."

"What's that?" I ask warily.

"Fermented soybean. It stinks like… I can't even describe it."

I shake my head. "You're evil."

"I know," she says gleefully. "So, how's Ginger?"

"Stella's great." I smile and rest my hand on my cheek.

She shakes her head. "You're gross when you're in love."

Before I can reply, a voice calls out somewhere off screen to her side. She sighs. "I gotta go, Zel. Time to make some yen. Talk soon." She grins and waves, and she's gone.

I smile and shut down my computer.

I guess you can tell Prim and I are okay now. A few weeks after I sent the album, she magically appeared on Skype. And she was the same Prim she used to be. We didn't talk about everything that had happened or anything that she had confessed to me. And we still don't. If she ever wanted to, I'd be there for her, but it's not like I expected Prim to change. Just because she put her feelings out loud and on the line once doesn't mean she's about to make a habit of it.

I just hold tight to the knowledge of how far she went past her safety zone because she needs me in her life. Because she values me—and us—that much. And since she never treated me badly before that, I let her be the person she is— recalcitrant and, well, *Prim-ish*.

So when she Skypes me from her teeny shared apartments in cities like Tokyo and Los Angeles and bitches loud and long about the ridiculousness of being a model, I just laugh and listen. When she sends me a photo of a dog turd on the footpath outside a Givenchy shop in Paris, I stick it to my wall. And when she refuses to meet Stella but demands to see a video of her dancing, I show her. Because she's Prim, and she doesn't change. And if this is how she needs to be to exist in the world, then this is how it is. And in return, she gifts me with her utter faith in me and with her delightful way of remaking the world into a warped, hilarious version of itself.

We're staying in Sydney now. Dad's been offered another contract before he even finished this one. He'll do his short job in New York, and then he'll come right back to the theatre company. Mum and Dad like it here. They like the weather and their jobs. I like it too.

I know, I *know*. I insisted at the start of all this that I would never change my mind about wanting to go back to New York. But I like to think I am the kind of person who can admit when I'm wrong. I like Sydney now. I have sunshine and photography. We have plans for bigger and better drama projects. I have my friends, pack of geeks that we are. I have Stella. Home is where the people are, right?

The only thing missing is Prim. But even if I never go back to New York, I know Prim and I will be friends forever. Because here's the thing I've figured out: try and keep everybody you love in your life if you can, even the difficult ones. Even when it gets hard. Because if you ever thought they were worth it at some point, they probably are. You just have to figure out where they fit.

~ ~ ~

About Emily O'Beirne

Thirteen-year-old Emily woke up one morning with a sudden itch to write her first novel. All day, she sat through her classes, feverishly scribbling away (her rare silence probably a cherished respite for her teachers). And by the time the last bell rang, she had penned fifteen handwritten pages of angsty drivel, replete with blood-red sunsets, moody saxophone music playing somewhere far off in the night, and abandoned whiskey bottles rolling across tables. Needless to say, that singular literary accomplishment is buried in a box somewhere, ready for her later amusement.

From Melbourne, Australia, Emily was recently granted her PhD. She works part-time in academia, where she hates marking papers but loves working with her students. She also loves where she lives but travels as much as possible and tends to harbour crushes on cities more than on people.

CONNECT WITH EMILY:

Website: www.emilyobeirne.com

OTHER BOOKS FROM YLVA PUBLISHING

www.ylva-publishing.com

Points of Departure

Emily O'Beirne

ISBN: 978-3-95533-698-1
Length: 251 pages (90,000 words)

Best friends Kit and Liza have been looking forward to this trip forever. Five girls, five tickets overseas. But when Kit has to drop out, Liza's left with three girls she barely knows. While Kit's stuck at home, Liza's exploring Europe with sensible Tam, party girl Mai, and miserable Olivia. And they're all learning that travel isn't just about the places you go, but about who you're with.

The Space Between

Michelle L. Teichman

ISBN: 978-3-95533-581-6
Length: 280 pages (92,000 words)

Life is easy for Harper, the most popular girl in her grade, until she meets Sarah, a friendless loner who only cares about art. Inexplicably, Harper can't stop thinking about her.

Unsure of her feelings for Harper, Sarah is afraid to act on what her heart is telling her. She can't believe Harper feels the same.

Can Harper and Sarah find a way to be together, or will fear keep them apart forever?

The Light of the World

Ellen Simpson

ISBN: 978-3-95533-507-6

Length: 257 pages (107,000 words)

Confronted with a mystery upon her grandmother's death, Eva delves into the rich and complicated history of a woman who hid far more than a long-lost-love from the world. Darkness is lurking behind every corner, and someone is looking for the key to her grandmother's secrets; the light of the world.

Stowe Away

Blythe Rippon

ISBN: 978-3-95533-523-6

Length: 279 pages (97,500 words)

Brilliant, awkward Samantha Latham couldn't wait to leave rural Stowe for an illustrious career in medicine. But when an unexpected call from a hospital forces Sam to move back home to care for her ailing mother, a life of boredom and isolation seems imminent—until a charming restaurant owner named Maria inspires Sam to rethink everything she knows about Stowe, success, and above all, love.

COMING FROM YLVA PUBLISHING

www.ylva-publishing.com

Punk Like Me

(Punk Series)

revised edition

JD Glass

Nina, at 21, is standing at the edge of "being" and "becoming." She remembers when her parents, and the nuns, and everyone else seemed to have plans for her, of who she was and who she'd be. Her dad calls "punk" anything and anyone that disobeys the norms. And then there's Nina's feelings. Feelings for her friend Kerry, feelings from her friend, Samantha - and then there are decisions; decisions that will change the course of an entire life, single moments that stand alone and change everything.

Sometimes, you jump. Sometimes, you're pushed. And sometimes you have friends that won't let you fall.

Punk Like Me—it's not about breaking the rules: it's about following your heart.

Here's the Thing
© 2016 by Emily O'Beirne

ISBN: 978-3-95533-728-5

Also available as e-book.

Published by Ylva Publishing, legal entity of Ylva Verlag, e.Kfr.

Ylva Verlag, e.Kfr.
Owner: Astrid Ohletz
Am Kirschgarten 2
65830 Kriftel
Germany

www.ylva-publishing.com

First edition: 2016

Credits
Edited by Astrid Ohletz & Michelle Aguilar
Cover Design by Adam Lloyd